WINGS, WHEELS AND WATER
A FIRST BOOK OF TRANSPORT

Contents

Page 2
THINGS THAT FLY
Page 25
THINGS ON WHEELS
Page 49
THINGS THAT FLOAT

THINGS THAT FLY

Kate Little

Designed by Steve Page

Illustrated by Peter Bull and Guy Smith

Contents

2	All about aircraft	16	Wind power
4	How planes fly	18	First flyers
6	Airliners	20	Space flight
8	Aircraft engines	22	Biggest and fastest
10	At the airport	23	Air sports
12	Helicopters	24	Index
14	Lighter-than-air		

All about aircraft

This section of the book is about many different types of aircraft. It tells you how they fly and what powers them – pushing or pulling them through the air. You can also find out what happens at an airport, how planes take-off and land, and about the special spacecraft which fly in Space.

▲
A helicopter can hover in one place in the air. Find out how on page 12.

This is a bi-plane. You can see what the first bi-plane looked like on page 18.
▼

▲
This hot-air balloon is known as a lighter-than-air craft. See why on page 14.

▲
Page 20 shows you what sort of engine a rocket has and how it works.

On pages 6 and 7 you ▶ can see what the inside of this Jumbo jet looks like.

Plane power

A glider stays in the air only when there are rising air currents to keep it up.

Powerful jet engines have increased the flying speed of many airliners to over 900km/h (569mph).

Rocket engines are like jet engines and push the rocket very fast out into space.

This plane is solar powered. Its engine gets its energy from the sun.

Parts of a plane

The ailerons, flaps, elevators, spoilers and rudder are all moving parts on the wings and tail of a plane which make it fly in different directions.

The flaps and spoilers help lift the plane into the air on take-off and also when coming down to land.

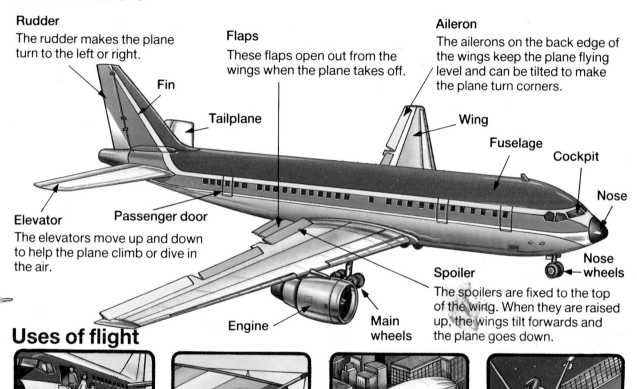

Rudder
The rudder makes the plane turn to the left or right.

Flaps
These flaps open out from the wings when the plane takes off.

Aileron
The ailerons on the back edge of the wings keep the plane flying level and can be tilted to make the plane turn corners.

Fin

Tailplane

Wing

Fuselage

Cockpit

Nose

Elevator
The elevators move up and down to help the plane climb or dive in the air.

Passenger door

Engine

Main wheels

Spoiler
The spoilers are fixed to the top of the wing. When they are raised up, the wings tilt forwards and the plane goes down.

Nose wheels

Uses of flight

Nowadays, many people travel by air. This Airbus can carry 200 passengers.

Hang gliding is a very popular sport. Experienced pilots can stay up in the air for hours.

Some airships are used for advertising, because they can fly very slowly.

Satellites above the Earth send back information about the weather, and relay television signals.

How planes fly

How does a plane lift off the ground? You need to know about the air to understand how this happens. Air moves around us all the time. It presses against us and has weight. You feel the weight of the air when the wind blows on your face. A plane stays up in the air because of the air rushing past its wings.

Wing experiment

To see how a wing lifts up, hold a thin strip of paper to your lips and blow hard over the top of it. It rises because there is less air on top and the air underneath pushes up.

Aerofoil

Plane wings are curved on top and flat underneath. This is an aerofoil shape. When a plane flies, air flows faster over the top of the wing, so there is less air pressure there. Stronger air pressure underneath pushes the wings up.

Drag

The force of the air pushing against the plane when it is flying forwards is called drag.

Forces on a plane

When a plane is flying, four forces keep it flying straight and level. These are lift and weight and thrust and drag.

Lift

Air rushing over the top of the wings and pushing from below lifts the plane.

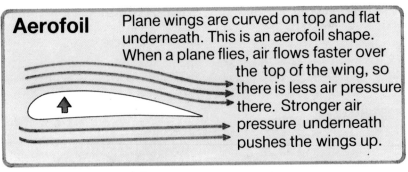

Lift

Drag

Thrust

Weight

Thrust

The propeller pulls the plane forwards through the air. This force is called thrust.

Weight

The weight of the plane pulls it down to balance against the lift.

How planes move about

A plane has to be able to turn, climb and dive. To do this, most planes are fitted with special hinged surfaces on the edges of the wings, tailplane and fins. The pilot uses special controls on the flight deck to move these.

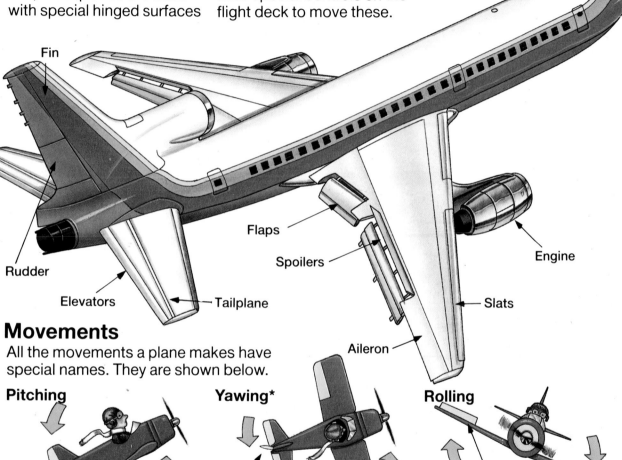

Fin

Rudder

Elevators

Tailplane

Flaps

Spoilers

Aileron

Engine

Slats

Movements

All the movements a plane makes have special names. They are shown below.

Pitching

Elevator

This is when the nose of the plane moves up or down. Moving the elevators on the tailplane makes the plane climb or dive.

Yawing*

Rudder

This is when the nose of the plane moves to the left or right. To make the plane yaw, the pilot moves the rudder.

Rolling

Ailerons

Moving the ailerons up and down on the trailing edge of the wings makes the plane roll from side to side.

*The plane in this picture is seen from above.

5

Airliners

Large airliners such as the Boeing 747 are designed to carry lots of passengers. The American Boeing 747 is the largest airliner in use today. It is called a Jumbo jet because of its size. It can carry up to 500 people, travel at 978km/h (608mph) at a height of 15km (9.3 miles), for 10,424km (6,477 miles).

Parts

Over 4.5 million separate parts make up one complete 747 airliner.

Boeing 747

Rudder

Elevator

Aluminium body

Seats

The 747 has room for 500 passengers, but usually carries 400 to give passengers extra room and comfort.

Seats

Body frame

Main landing wheels

Flaps

Landing wheels

On the ground, the 747 stands on two nose wheels and 16 main wheels. They all fold away after take-off.

The engines of a Jumbo jet burn more than 11,000kg (24,250lbs) of fuel every hour.

Turbofan engine

Cargo 747

This 747 has been adapted to carry only cargo. The nose of the plane swings upwards so large boxes can be loaded at the front. It can carry up to 130 tonnes (127 tons).

The 747 has a wing span of 59.6m (195ft 9in) and is 70.7m (232ft) long and 19.3m (63ft 4in) high. It is a wide-bodied airliner and ten seats can be put side by side across the cabin. With passengers and cargo, the 747 weighs nearly 406 tonnes (400 tons).

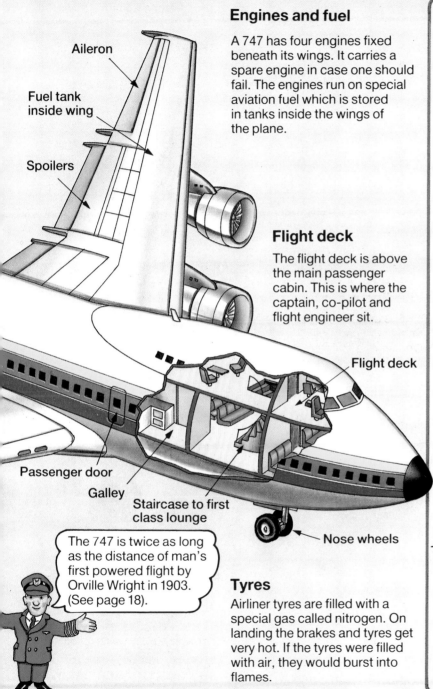

Engines and fuel

A 747 has four engines fixed beneath its wings. It carries a spare engine in case one should fail. The engines run on special aviation fuel which is stored in tanks inside the wings of the plane.

Aileron

Fuel tank inside wing

Spoilers

Flight deck

The flight deck is above the main passenger cabin. This is where the captain, co-pilot and flight engineer sit.

Flight deck

Passenger door

Galley

Staircase to first class lounge

The 747 is twice as long as the distance of man's first powered flight by Orville Wright in 1903. (See page 18).

Nose wheels

Tyres

Airliner tyres are filled with a special gas called nitrogen. On landing the brakes and tyres get very hot. If the tyres were filled with air, they would burst into flames.

Wing shapes

Planes have different shaped wings. The shape is important because it changes how fast the plane can fly.

Swept wings

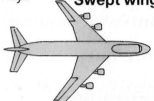

Most airliners like the 747 have a swept wing formation. This gives them greater speed.

Straight wings

Small, light aircraft have straight, thick wings. They fly at low speeds for short distances.

Delta wings

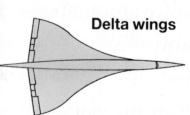

Concorde has delta-shaped wings so it can travel at twice the speed of sound. It has a top speed of 2,032km/h (1,300mph).

Aircraft engines

All modern airliners are powered by jet engines. Early planes had piston engines like the engine in a car. They ran on petrol and the engine turned a propeller which pulled the plane through the air. A jet engine sucks in air at the front and pushes it out faster at the back. This moves the plane forwards.

The jet engine

Jet engines burn a fuel called kerosene. This produces hot gases which are thrust out of the exhaust at great speed, pushing the plane forwards.

Jet powered balloon

To see how a jet engine works, blow up a balloon and hold it at the neck. Air is held inside, pushing out on all sides. If you let go, the air will rush out of the neck and the balloon will shoot forwards.

The first jet

The Heinkel He 178 was designed by a German, Ernst Heinkel, in 1939. It was the first plane to fly powered by a jet engine.

Compressor

The compressor is a number of blades shaped like aerofoils. These blades turn round quickly and suck air into the engine.

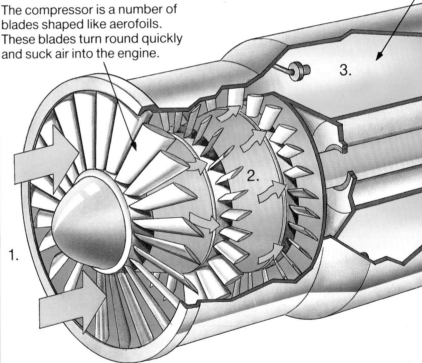

1. When the engine is on the blades turn round very fast and pull air into the engine.

2. The air gets very hot travelling fast along this tube before it goes into the combustion chamber.

Combustion chamber

This is where the air and fuel burns explosively to produce hot gases.

Turbine

The hot gases from the combustion chamber turn the turbine blades round. The turbine turns the compressor which sucks in more air to keep the engine running.

Exhaust tail-pipe

This is where the exhaust gases are pushed out of the engine.

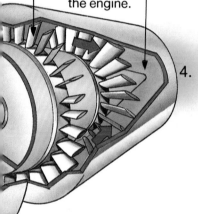

4.

3. Kerosene is sprayed into the combustion chamber and mixes with air. The mixture is lit by a spark and explodes, producing very hot gases.

4. The hot gases are pushed past the turbine wheel and rush out of the exhaust tail-pipe very fast.

Types of jets

Below are four different types of jet engines. They all power different types of aircraft.

Turbojet

Turbojets are very noisy ▶ because the exhaust gases rush out of the tail-pipe very fast. Concorde has turbojet engines.

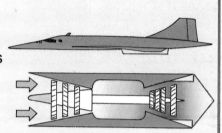

Turbofan

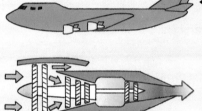

◀ A Jumbo jet has turbofan engines. They are less noisy and use less fuel than turbojets. A turbofan has two compressors. The front one, called a fan, also acts as a propeller pulling the plane forwards.

Turboprop

A turboprop is designed to ▶ turn propellers to pull the plane through the air. Slower flying planes use these engines.

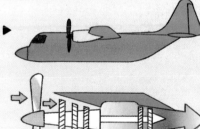

Turboshaft

◀ Turboshaft engines are usually fitted to helicopters. The engine turns both the main and tail rotor blades.

At the airport

The first airports were open fields with tents for travellers and hangars for the planes. Today, most international airports are as big as a small city. Thousands of people are needed to keep the airport running. They work in shops and restaurants, as baggage handlers, cleaners, engineers and customs officers.

Control tower

◄ The control tower overlooks the runways. Inside, air traffic controllers direct planes when they are landing, taking off and moving about on the apron. They have to know where each plane is to avoid a crash.

Apron
Around the airport terminals is the apron, where the planes are loaded, unloaded and refuelled.

Passenger terminal

Baggage truck

Luggage is loaded on to a baggage truck.

Passenger terminal

This is where everyone comes to check in for their flight and send luggage ahead to the plane. There are shops, banks and restaurants and information about aircraft arrivals and departures.

Fuel tanker
The plane is refuelled from a tanker

Ground services

Once a plane has landed, the ground services move in quickly to prepare the plane for its next flight.

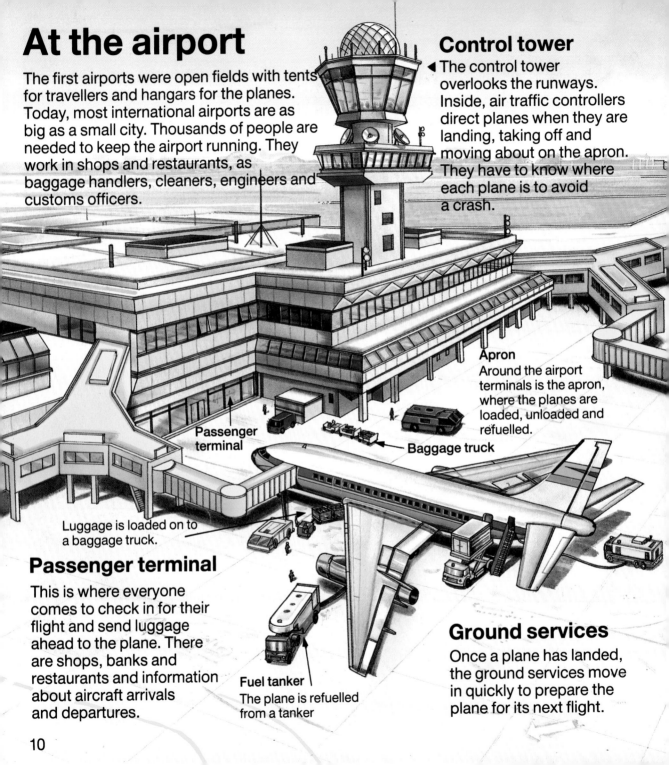

Landing

Planes coming in to land must have permission from the approach controller in the tower. Pilots radio in many miles before reaching the runway.

Runway

Taxiway

Stacking

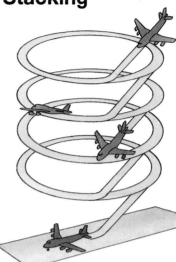

When there are several planes waiting to land, they form a stack in the air. The planes circle one above the other, about 305m (1,000ft) apart.

Take-off

Before take-off, the pilot gives his flight plan to the air departure controller.

The taxiways are clearly marked with lines to show the pilot exactly where he must position the plane on approaching the runway.

Runway

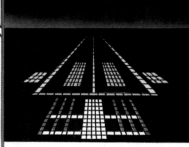

At night, bright lights and white markers on the runways and taxiways guide the pilots in to land and before take-off.

The flight plan

The flight plan gives details of the plane's destination and the height and speed it will travel at. The controller checks the plan carefully to make sure the plane flies well clear of other planes.

Helicopters

Helicopters are VTOL (vertical take-off and landing) aircraft. This means they can take off and land in a small space. Helicopters can hover in the air, fly forwards, backwards and sideways.

The rotor blades on a helicopter are aerofoil shaped, like the wings of a plane. (See page 4). When they spin round fast, the helicopter lifts off the ground.

Rotor blades

Rotor blades →

Engine →

Rotor blades
These controls tilt the rotor blades forwards and backwards. This lets the helicopter fly in any direction.

Rudder pedals
The rudder pedals control the tail rotor blades.

Landing skid

Flying a helicopter

Hovering

When the rotor blades are spinning round fast and are kept level, the helicopter will hover in one spot in the air.

Going forwards

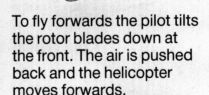

To fly forwards the pilot tilts the rotor blades down at the front. The air is pushed back and the helicopter moves forwards.

Going backwards

To fly backwards the pilot tilts the rotor blades back. Air is pulled in front of the helicopter, moving it backwards.

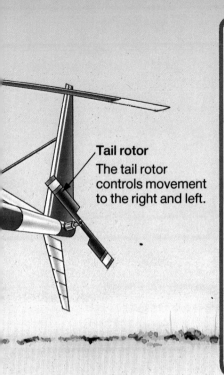

Tail rotor
The tail rotor controls movement to the right and left.

Jump jets

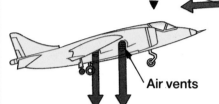

Vents point downwards on take-off and landing. ▼

Vents point backwards for normal flight. ▲

Air vents

The Harrier jump jet can also take-off and land vertically. Its powerful engine forces its exhaust gases out through air vents. On take-off, the vents point downwards. The downward force of the exhaust gases pushes the plane off the ground. The vents then swivel round and the gases are thrust backwards, shooting the jet forwards.

Useful helicopters

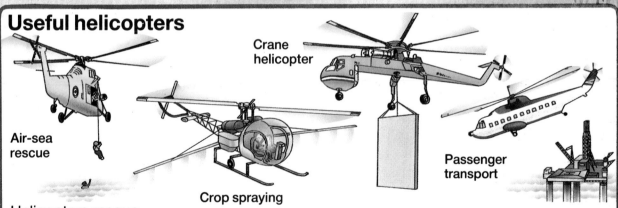

Crane helicopter

Air-sea rescue

Crop spraying

Passenger transport

Helicopters rescue people at sea. They have winches and strong steel cables joined to harnesses, to lift people out of the water.

Some farmers spray their crops using specially adapted helicopters. They can fly slowly over the fields.

This helicopter is carrying a heavy load to a building site that cannot be reached in any other way.

Workers on oil rigs out at sea have to be taken to work by helicopter. An oil rig has a small landing pad for helicopters.

Lighter-than-air

The flying things on these pages are not like normal aircraft. They are known as lighter-than-air craft. They do not have wings, but are filled with gas or hot air to lift them off the ground.

The first balloon

Their first passengers were a duck, a rooster and a sheep.

The Montgolfiers, two French brothers, invented the first hot-air balloon in 1783. They watched smoke rising from a fire and decided they could make other things rise in smoke.

Hot-air balloons

Balloons were the first aircraft that people flew in. The first ones were filled with hot air. Later, they were filled with gas that was lighter than air to make them fly.

Nylon Material

Gas burner

Ropes

Basket

How hot-air balloons fly

The balloon is inflated by blowing hot air into the bag using a gas burner. Hot air is lighter than cool air, so the balloon will rise.

To keep the balloon in the air, the air inside it is kept hot with short bursts of flame. Balloons cannot be steered. They go where the wind blows them.

To descend, the pilot lets the air inside the balloon cool. It gets heavier, so the balloon drops. On the ground, the pilot lets the last of the hot air out.

Airships

The first airships were shaped balloons with steam engines fitted to them. The engine turned a propeller which pulled the airship through the air. They were filled with a gas which was lighter than air, called hydrogen.

A Zeppelin airship

Upper and lower rudders

Rigid airships like this one were over 200m (656 ft) long.

Gas bags inside the framework were filled with hydrogen gas.

Steel framework

Propeller

This airship had five propellers.

Engine and propeller

Passenger cabin

The outside skin was made of linen material.

The first airship

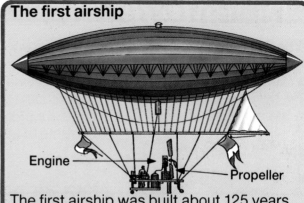

Engine

Propeller

The first airship was built about 125 years ago by a Frenchman called Henri Giffard. It was 43.5m (143 feet) long and was powered by a small steam engine. It could be steered through light winds.

The airship was fixed to a mooring mast by steel wires attached to the nose.

Fuel and water tanks

Navigation and control cabin (gondola)

Blimps

This blimp is the sort of airship you see today. They sometimes carry television cameras to film football matches, other sports and news events.

Rigid airships

Count Zeppelin, a German, was a famous inventor of rigid airships from 1900. His airships had metal frames. Inside these were bags of hydrogen. Many of the airships carried people from Germany to America. They stopped flying because the hydrogen gas often caught fire.

Wind power

The flying things on these pages do not have engines. When people first tried to fly, they fixed wings to their arms and jumped from steep hills. From this idea, the first gliders were designed and built. People were only able to travel a very short way. Modern gliders can fly for hours if there are plenty of air currents to keep them up.

Tailplane

Modern gliders

Modern gliders are made of very light materials like plywood and fibreglass.

Rudder

Cockpit

The body is narrow to cut through the air easily. The wings are long and thin to give plenty of lift. A glider needs more lift from the aerofoil wings because it has no engine.

Launching a glider

Tow cable

A glider is towed into the air by another plane or behind a car. When it is high enough, the tow cable is released and the glider flies on its own.

Flying a glider

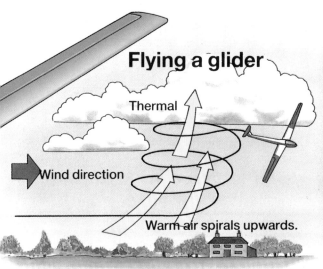

Thermal

Wind direction

Warm air spirals upwards.

To stay up in the air, the pilot has to find places where warm air rises. Rising warm air currents are called thermals. A skilled pilot will know where to find thermals and can spiral upwards with the air currents.

Hang gliders

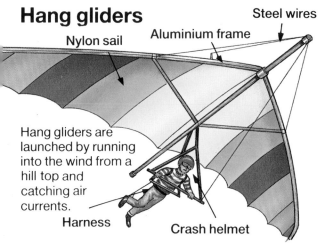

Steel wires

Nylon sail

Aluminium frame

Hang gliders are launched by running into the wind from a hill top and catching air currents.

Harness

Crash helmet

A hang glider is like a large kite which supports the weight of a person. It is made from a nylon sail and a light aluminium frame. The pilot hangs from the frame in a harness and steers by swinging his body about under the sail.

Parachutes

Today, parachute jumping is a very popular sport. This square-rig parachute can move forwards at about 40km/h (25mph) and can be steered so the jumper can land on a target.

Parachute descent

The jumper leaps from a plane with a parachute pack on his back. He pulls a cord and the canopy ▶ comes out.

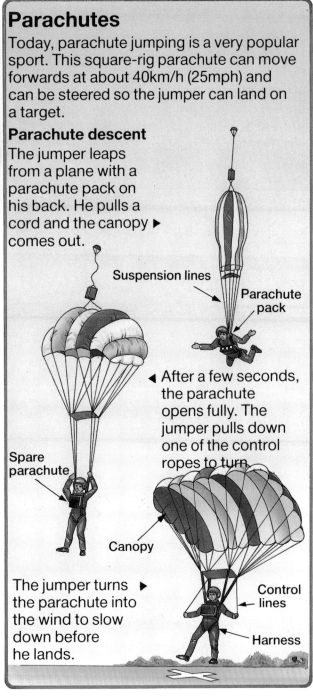

Suspension lines

Parachute pack

◀ After a few seconds, the parachute opens fully. The jumper pulls down one of the control ropes to turn.

Spare parachute

Canopy

The jumper turns ▶ the parachute into the wind to slow down before he lands.

Control lines

Harness

First flyers

Less than 100 years ago no one had ever flown in a powered plane and only very few people had flown in a glider (see page 17). This page tells you about the first planes and what made them fly. On the opposite page you can find out about some famous first flights.

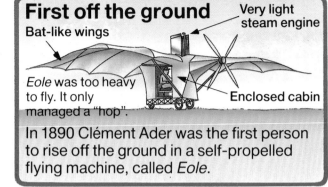

First off the ground

Bat-like wings

Very light steam engine

Eole was too heavy to fly. It only managed a "hop".

Enclosed cabin

In 1890 Clément Ader was the first person to rise off the ground in a self-propelled flying machine, called *Eole*.

The *Flyer* ▶

The pilot worked control wires by moving his body from side to side.

Wings covered by muslin material.

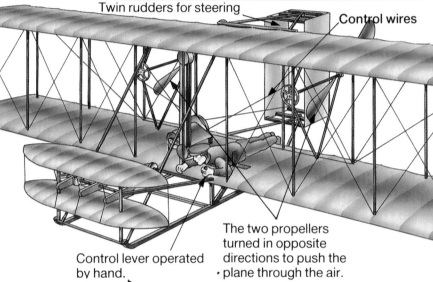

Twin rudders for steering

Control wires

The two propellers turned in opposite directions to push the plane through the air.

Control lever operated by hand.

First to fly

The first powered flight was in 1903, in an engine-driven plane built by Wilbur and Orville Wright. Their machine had two sets of wings, one above the other and was called a bi-plane.

Float-sea planes

Henri Fabre's float-sea plane

Glenn Curtiss' seaplane

A float-sea plane takes off and lands on water. The first one was flown by a Frenchman, Henri Fabre, in 1910. The next year an

American, Glenn Curtiss, flew a plane with floats as well as wheels. Nowadays, seaplanes are used all over the world.

The Wright Brothers' *Flyer* had no cabin. Instead the pilot controlled the machine from a lying down position on the lower wing.

Unlike the Wright Brothers, many early experimenters were killed because they did not know how to control their flying machines.

Famous flights

To the moon

◀ In 1969, the first men landed on the Moon. The American crew travelled there in the *Apollo XI* spacecraft.

First across water

Blériot flew his own plane, *Blériot XI.*

One of the most daring first flights was across the English Channel. A Frenchman, Louis Blériot, achieved this in 1909.

Crossing the Atlantic
▲

In 1927, an American, Charles Lindbergh, made the first non-stop solo flight across the Atlantic, in 33 hours and 39 minutes.

Round the World

Wiley Post, an American, ▶ was the first person ever to fly round the world. He did this between 15-22 July 1933.

Into space

◀ The first space journey was in 1961. A Russian cosmonaut, Yuri Gagarin, travelled in the spacecraft, *Vostok 1.*

To Australia

The first solo flight from ▶ England to Australia was made by a woman pilot, Amy Johnson in 1930. She flew a de Havilland Gypsy Moth.

19

Space flight

Where is Space?

The Earth is surrounded by a layer of air, called the atmosphere. The further you go from the Earth, the thinner the atmosphere becomes, until it finally disappears. This is where Space begins.

Flying in space

An ordinary plane cannot fly in Space because its engines need air. A rocket carries all its fuel and oxidizer (to produce oxygen to make the fuel burn) with it into Space.

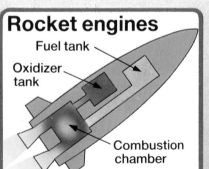

Rocket engines

Fuel tank

Oxidizer tank

Combustion chamber

Inside a rocket there are separate tanks of fuel and oxidizer. These mix together and burn, producing hot gases which rush out of the exhaust, thrusting the rocket up.

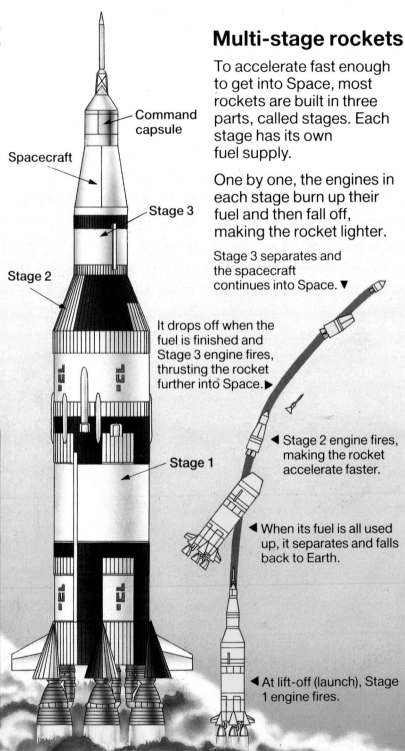

Command capsule

Spacecraft

Stage 3

Stage 2

Stage 1

Multi-stage rockets

To accelerate fast enough to get into Space, most rockets are built in three parts, called stages. Each stage has its own fuel supply.

One by one, the engines in each stage burn up their fuel and then fall off, making the rocket lighter.

Stage 3 separates and the spacecraft continues into Space. ▼

It drops off when the fuel is finished and Stage 3 engine fires, thrusting the rocket further into Space.▶

◀ Stage 2 engine fires, making the rocket accelerate faster.

◀ When its fuel is all used up, it separates and falls back to Earth.

◀ At lift-off (launch), Stage 1 engine fires.

Satellites

A satellite is an object which flies round (orbits) a larger object, like a planet.

Satellites are launched into orbit from rockets.

Communications satellite

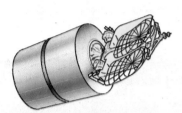

This type of satellite enables you to telephone right across the world.

Weather satellite

Weather satellites collect information which is used to forecast the weather.

The Space Shuttle

The American Space Shuttle is different from an ordinary rocket because it can be used again. When it returns to Earth, it lands on a runway like a plane.

Into Space and into orbit

There is a force all around Earth called gravity which keeps things on the ground. When you throw a ball into the air, it comes down again. Gravity pulls it back to Earth. Getting past gravity is the hardest part of a space journey. A rocket must travel very fast to get into Space and launch a satellite into orbit.

▲ A rocket travelling faster than 40,000km/h (24,856mph) will shoot out into Space.

▲ A satellite launched from a rocket at about 29,000km/h (18,020mph) will go into orbit around the Earth.

◀ A rocket flying at less than 29,000km/h (18.020mph) cannot escape Earth's gravity and it will fall back to Earth.

Biggest and fastest

On this page are some of the world's biggest and fastest planes. The biggest commercial airliner is the Jumbo jet which you can see on pages 6 and 7. In 1974 a Jumbo carried 674 passengers to safety from a cyclone in Australia.

The biggest

Lockheed C-5A Galaxy (America)

This is the biggest transport plane in the world. It can carry two tanks, 270 soldiers and lots of machinery.

Mil Mi-12 (Russia)

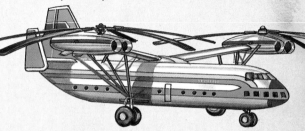

This is the world's largest helicopter. It has four engines and it weighs 105 tonnes (103.3 tons).

Graf Zeppelin II (Germany)

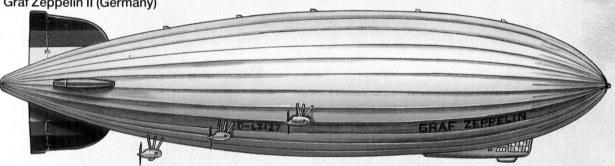

This was the biggest rigid airship ever built. It was 245m (803.8 feet) long. This is about the same length as three and a half Jumbo jets standing nose to tail.

The fastest

Concorde

Concorde is the fastest airliner in the world. It flies at 2,333km/h (1,450mph) which is over twice the speed of sound.

Lockheed SR-71

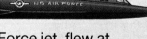

This United States Air Force jet, flew at 3,529.5km/h (2,193.2mph). This is about 13 times faster than the fastest car on the road.

Air sports

At most air shows today you will see displays of aerobatics, or stunt flying. Pilots turn and twist their planes about in the sky.

Aerobatics

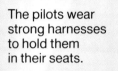

The pilots wear strong harnesses to hold them in their seats.

Famous flyer

In 1934, Geoffrey Tyson, a famous barnstormer, flew across the English Channel upside down.

Aerobatics began after the First World War. Pilots travelled in flying circuses performing daring stunts in the sky. In America, they were called barnstormers.

Air racing

Air racing is one of the fastest sports. In a race, eight planes fly around a course marked by pylons. The race includes take-off and landing.

Formation flying

Some groups, like the French Air Force's *Patrouille de France,* fly in formation at air shows all over Europe. The team of nine fly close together and cross flight paths at great speed, trailing streams of coloured smoke. They are very skilled pilots.

Aircraft words

Here are some special words about aircraft which have been used in this section of the book, and others you may have heard.

Plane parts

The wings, tailplane and fins of a plane are fitted with special hinged surfaces which allow the plane to turn, climb and dive.

The **ailerons** and **rudder** make the plane turn to the right and left.

The **spoilers** and **elevators** make the plane climb and dive.

Movements

The movements a plane makes have special names.

Pitching is when the nose of the plane moves up or down.

Yawing is when the nose of the plane moves to the left or right.

Rolling is when the wings of the plane tip from side to side.

Supersonic

Airliners that fly faster than the speed of sound are called supersonic. Concorde flies at twice the speed of sound. When it is flying at top speed, you hear it long after it has passed overhead.

Wing shapes

Aircraft wings have different shapes depending how fast the plane has to fly.

Small, light aircraft have thick, **straight** wings and fly quite slowly.

Most jet airliners have **swept** wings for speed.

Supersonic jets, like Concorde, have **delta** shaped wings so they can fly faster than the speed of sound.

Automatic pilot

All commercial airliners are fitted with an 'automatic pilot'. This is an electronic control system which keeps the aircraft on a fixed course at a set height and speed. The 'automatic pilot' can land the plane in fog.

Radar

Radar screens are used in the control tower to show the position of all aircraft approaching or leaving an airport. The planes appear as a dot on the screen. Airliners are fitted with radar screens too, so the pilot can pinpoint his position even in clouds and fog.

Flight instruments

The flight deck of an airliner has lots of controls, dials and switches. Here are some important dials which the pilot checks regularly.

The **altimeter** shows the plane's altitude, or height above the ground.

The **compass** shows the direction in which the plane is flying. The pilot sets a course from this.

The **artificial horizon** shows whether the plane is flying level.

THINGS ON WHEELS

Kate Little

Designed by Steve Page

Illustrated by Peter Bull

Contents

26 Going places on wheels
28 Parts of the car
30 How an engine works
32 On the road
34 Grand Prix racing
36 Motor sports
38 Off the road

40 Bicycles
41 Motorbikes
42 Types of trains
44 Trains today
46 Fastest on wheels
48 Car words

Going places on wheels

This book is all about different types of things on wheels. It shows what the very first bicycles, motorbikes, cars and trains looked like and explains how they work. You can also find out about different types of racing vehicles.

On page 40 you can see the differences between an old-fashioned high-wheeled bicycle and a modern bicycle.

These are the working parts of a car. You can find out how they work on pages 30-33.

You can find out how this train works on page 44.

The very first motorbike was made of wood. On page 41 you can see how much they have changed.

This is a Formula 1 racing car. Find out about other motor sports on page 36.

The wheel story

Before wheels were invented, tree trunks were used as rollers to help push heavy loads along the ground.

The first wheels were made of solid wood about 6,000 years ago. Later, they were fixed to carts pulled by horses and oxen.

Then wheels were made with wooden spokes, which made them lighter. An iron rim round the edge made them last longer.

What makes them go ?

Person power

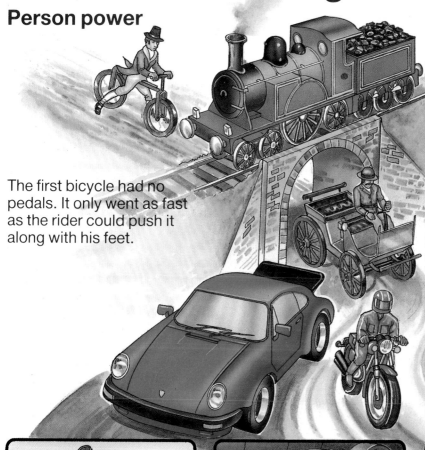

The first bicycle had no pedals. It only went as fast as the rider could push it along with his feet.

Steam engines

Steam trains burned coal or wood. The fire heated a tank of water. Steam from this pushed a rod which made the wheels turn round.

Petrol power

The engine in a car and a motorbike is called the internal combustion engine. It burns petrol inside it to make the wheels turn.

The first four-wheeled car was a horse-drawn carriage with an engine fitted to it. It was built in 1886 by a German called Gottlieb Daimler.

Later, wheels were made with metal spokes. They were much stronger and lighter, so were good for bicycle wheels.

Train wheels are made of very strong steel. They have a ridge on the inside to stop them running off the track.

All car and bicycle wheels have air filled (pneumatic) tyres. These make riding over bumps in the road more comfortable.

Parts of the car

In a car factory, all the pieces needed to make a car are arranged in order. As each car moves along a line, all the parts are fitted to it. This is called an assembly line. At the end the car is finished and needs to be tested for any faults.

These strong steel bars lower the car body down on to the chassis.

The chassis

The engine, clutch and gearbox, driveshaft, rear axle, rear differential and suspension are all supported in a steel frame called the chassis. (This has been left out of the picture to make it clearer).

The engine is cased in and fitted to the front of the car.

The driveshaft joins the engine and gearbox to the rear axle.

Engine

Gearstick

Gearbox

Bumper

Radiator

Clutch

The clutch and the gearbox allow the car to be driven at different speeds and to go backwards.

Lights

The car body

The car body is made out of a big sheet of steel. The shape is pressed out by a huge machine which cuts out spaces for the doors and windows.

Accessories

The steering wheel, windscreen, lights, seats and bumpers are called accessories and are all added to the car at the end of the assembly line.

The suspension, these strong coil springs, helps keep the car level when going over bumps in the road.

The wheels are fixed to the rear axle.

Driveshaft

The differential connects the driveshaft to the rear axle.

Seat

Steering wheel

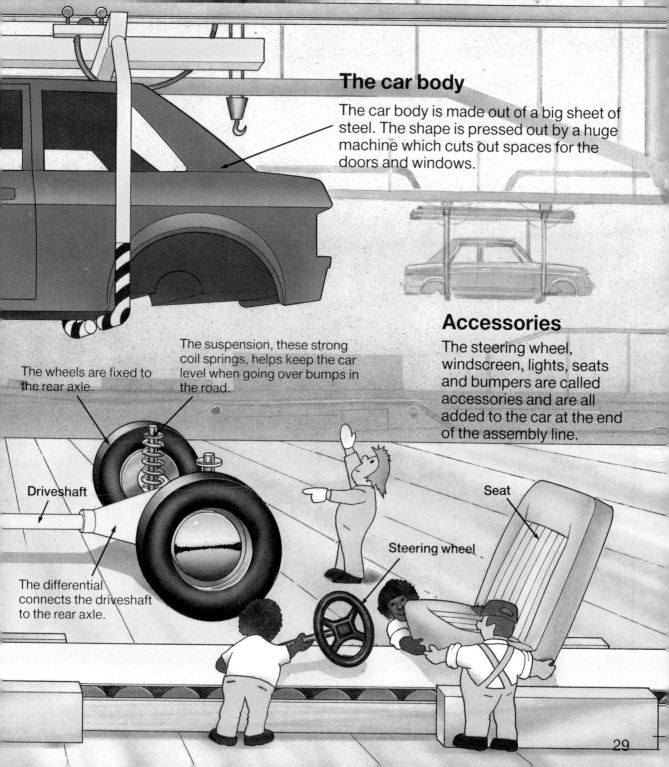

How an engine works

A car engine has many different moving parts that need to be kept oiled to keep it working well. Car engines run on a mixture of petrol and air which burns explosively inside the engine.

When the engine is switched on, the pistons move up and down inside the cylinders. This up and down movement turns the crankshaft round. The crankshaft turns the driveshaft, which makes the wheels go round.

Spark plug

Cylinder

Piston

Carburettor

Radiator

Crankshaft

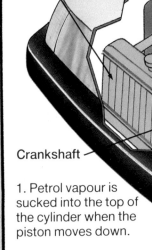

The carburettor

Petrol is mixed with air in the carburettor before it goes into the cylinder.

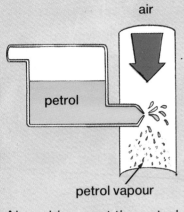

air

petrol

petrol vapour

Air rushing past the petrol breaks it up into tiny droplets so small you cannot see them. This is called petrol vapour.

1. Petrol vapour is sucked into the top of the cylinder when the piston moves down.

2. The piston moves up and squeezes the petrol vapour into a small space in the top of the cylinder.

3. An electric spark from the spark plug sets light to the petrol vapour. It explodes, pushing the piston down.

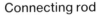

Connecting rod

4. Exhaust fumes are pushed out along the exhaust pipe by the piston moving up.

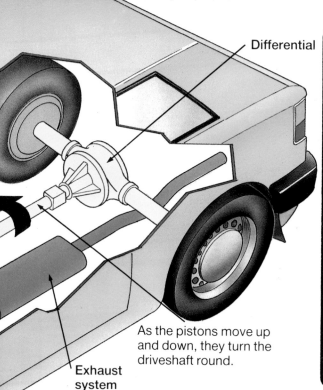

Differential

As the pistons move up and down, they turn the driveshaft round.

Exhaust system

This engine has four cylinders. More powerful engines have as many as six or 12 cylinders.

Piston power

The force that fires a cannonball from a cannon is similar to the force which pushes the pistons in the cylinders. When the gunpowder is lit, it explodes and hot gases force the ball out.

Driving the rear wheels ★

At the end of the driveshaft is a cogged wheel or gear which connects to a larger gear on the rear axle.

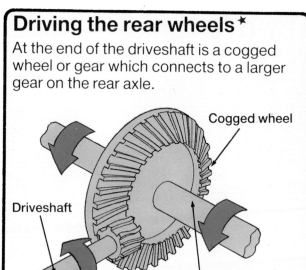

Cogged wheel

Driveshaft

Rear axle

The teeth of one gear fit into the other to make it turn. This makes the power from the engine drive the rear axle and rear wheels.

Hot engines

The radiator is a narrow metal box which contains water. Water is pumped around the engine to keep it cool.

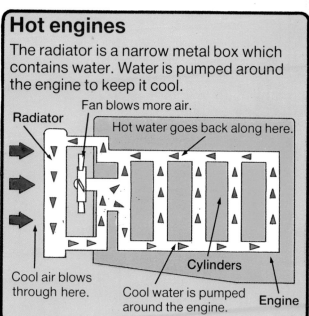

Fan blows more air.

Radiator

Hot water goes back along here.

Cool air blows through here.

Cool water is pumped around the engine.

Cylinders

Engine

★This picture is simplified. There are actually many more gear wheels in this part, (the "differential") to allow the rear wheels to go at different speeds round corners.

On the road

On these pages you can find out how the clutch and gears make the car go at different speeds and how the brakes work.

What are gears?

Gears are cogged wheels which fit together and turn at different speeds depending on the number of teeth they have.

This gear has 10 teeth.

This gear has 20 teeth.

The small one turns twice as fast as the big one.

Gear stick

Gearbox

Brake pedal

Most cars have four forward gears and one reverse. Trucks can have as many as 16 gears.

How the gearbox works

The top row of gears inside the gearbox are turned by the engine. They turn the bottom row, which make the wheels go round.

Most cars have drum brakes on rear wheels.

Using the gears

When starting off, the driver puts the engine into first gear. It needs a lot of power to get the car moving.

Second and third gear help the car to gain speed.

Fourth gear is used for driving along at a fast, steady speed.

Reverse gear changes the direction of the wheels so the car goes backwards.

How the clutch works

To change gear the driver has to press the clutch pedal down. This separates the two discs and stops the engine from turning the wheels.

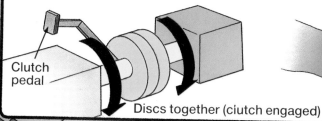

Clutch pedal

Discs together (clutch engaged)

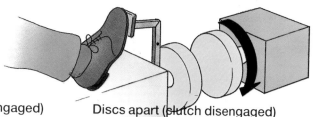

Discs apart (clutch disengaged)

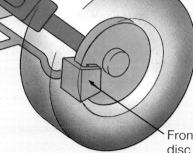

Front brakes are usually disc brakes.

Steering a car

Steering is worked by gears too. Instead of two cogged wheels there is a rack and a pinion.

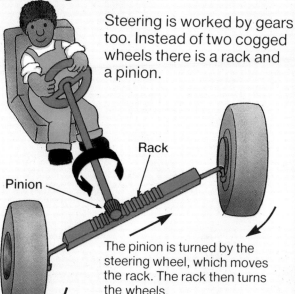

Pinion

Rack

The pinion is turned by the steering wheel, which moves the rack. The rack then turns the wheels.

How the brakes work

When the driver presses the brake pedal, pads are forced to rub against all four wheels. When they rub together, a force called friction stops them moving. Friction between the brakes and the wheels makes a car slow down.

Drum brakes

The brake drum is fixed inside the wheel. So when the brake shoes press out against the drum, the wheels slow down and stop.

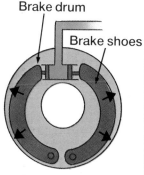

Brake drum

Brake shoes

Disc brakes

A steel disc is fixed inside the wheel. When the brake pads press in on the disc, friction stops the wheel moving.

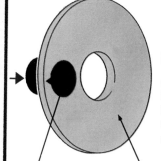

Brake pads

Steel disc

Grand Prix racing

Winning the Grand Prix Championship is the greatest achievement of all motor racing. Drivers and cars battle for ten months of the year on race tracks all over the world. They cover 5,470km (3,400 miles) during the 16 Grand Prix races. The drivers score points if they are among the first six to finish each race. There are two world championships, one for the cars and one for the drivers.

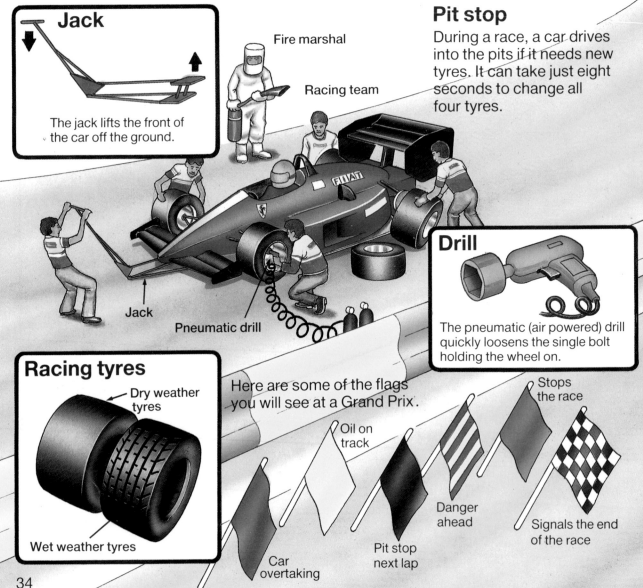

Jack

The jack lifts the front of the car off the ground.

Fire marshal

Racing team

Pit stop

During a race, a car drives into the pits if it needs new tyres. It can take just eight seconds to change all four tyres.

Drill

The pneumatic (air powered) drill quickly loosens the single bolt holding the wheel on.

Jack

Pneumatic drill

Racing tyres

Dry weather tyres

Wet weather tyres

Here are some of the flags you will see at a Grand Prix.

Oil on track

Stops the race

Danger ahead

Car overtaking

Pit stop next lap

Signals the end of the race

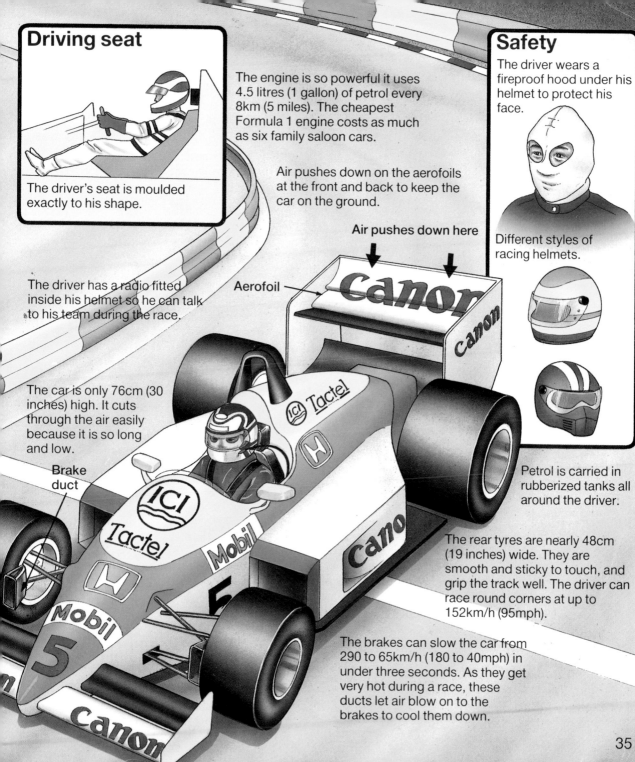

Driving seat

The driver's seat is moulded exactly to his shape.

The engine is so powerful it uses 4.5 litres (1 gallon) of petrol every 8km (5 miles). The cheapest Formula 1 engine costs as much as six family saloon cars.

Air pushes down on the aerofoils at the front and back to keep the car on the ground.

Air pushes down here

The driver has a radio fitted inside his helmet so he can talk to his team during the race.

Aerofoil

The car is only 76cm (30 inches) high. It cuts through the air easily because it is so long and low.

Brake duct

Safety

The driver wears a fireproof hood under his helmet to protect his face.

Different styles of racing helmets.

Petrol is carried in rubberized tanks all around the driver.

The rear tyres are nearly 48cm (19 inches) wide. They are smooth and sticky to touch, and grip the track well. The driver can race round corners at up to 152km/h (95mph).

The brakes can slow the car from 290 to 65km/h (180 to 40mph) in under three seconds. As they get very hot during a race, these ducts let air blow on to the brakes to cool them down.

Motor sports

There are many types of motor sports. Here are just three of them. The cars are all different and have been specially prepared in some way for their particular sport.

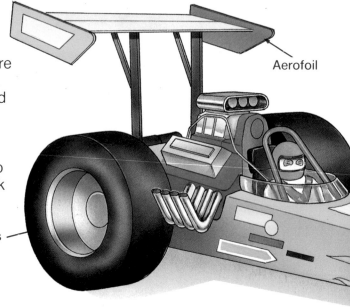

Aerofoil

Drag racing

Drag racing is a test of speed between two dragster cars. They race on a straight track over 400m (1/4 of a mile).

Slicks

A drag race

The driver makes the rear tyres spin round. This makes them hot and sticky so the car gets a good grip on the track when starting.

In just two seconds the car accelerates from 0 to 160km/h (0 to 100mph).

At the finish it is travelling at 320km/h (200mph).

Parachutes help slow the car down.

Start

Finish

Stock car racing

In stock car racing, old cars are raced on oval shaped dirt tracks.

Different classes of races are held for different types of cars.

All windows and back seats are taken out for safety.

Powerful brakes, suspension and engine are fitted.

Safety

Roll bar

Safety harness

Safety harness and roll bar protect the driver if the car turns over.

Slingshot dragster

The rear tyres, called slicks, have no tread and are made of very soft rubber. The front wheels are very light and thin, like bicycle wheels.

The high aerofoil at the back and the one between the front wheels stop the car lifting off the ground.

Aerofoil

Funny cars

This dragster is called a Funny Car. It has a top speed of 418km/h (260mph). To make the car go fast it burns rocket fuel in its engine.

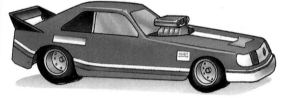

This old Ford Anglia has been fitted with a special engine and fat rear tyres to race in a mixed class.

Rallying

Rallies are held on snowy mountain roads, across rough country and through deserts all over the world.

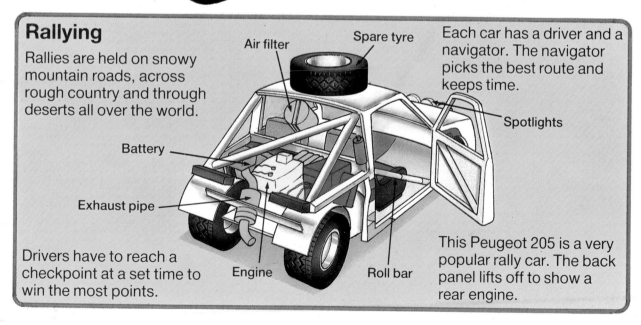

Air filter

Spare tyre

Each car has a driver and a navigator. The navigator picks the best route and keeps time.

Spotlights

Battery

Exhaust pipe

Engine

Roll bar

Drivers have to reach a checkpoint at a set time to win the most points.

This Peugeot 205 is a very popular rally car. The back panel lifts off to show a rear engine.

Off the road

Some cars are specially designed to travel over very rugged ground where there are no roads. An ordinary car is designed to run on good roads and would soon break down in conditions like these. The exhaust pipe would be knocked off, the tyres would burst and it could not go through rivers.

'County' Station Wagon

The Land Rover was designed for driving in rough country. This one looks very much like the first Land Rover ever built in 1948. The design has not changed much because it is so good.

The car body is high off the ground. It is bolted together in sections, so it will not bend or twist.

Spare tyre

Front axle

Front differential

Rear axle

Folding side step

Tough aluminium body

Rear differential

Extra springy suspension cushions the driver and passengers from bumps.

Big, chunky tyres help the car grip uneven ground. They are made with very thick rubber so they will not split.

What is four wheel drive?

An ordinary car has one differential which drives either the front or the rear wheels. A four wheel drive car has a differential at the front and the back so the engine turns all four wheels. This means that four wheel drive vehicles travel well over mud, snow or sand.

Rear axle

Engine

Driveshaft

Rear differential

Front axle

Front differential

Tyres

Heavy duty tyres with deep tread for going over rocks and sand.

What can four wheel drive do?

These are some of the things that four wheel drive (4WD) cars can do.

This Land Rover can be driven through rivers up to 50cm (20in) deep.

This pick-up truck can climb very steep slopes because of the extra power in its wheels.

This jeep can be driven on steeply banked tracks without it tipping over.

Other 4WD vehicles

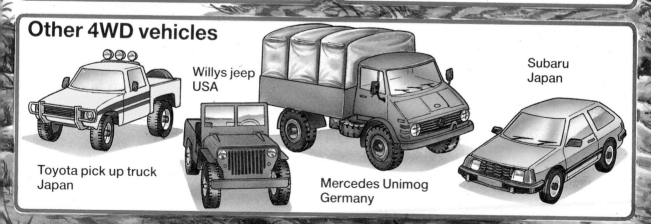

Willys jeep USA

Subaru Japan

Toyota pick up truck Japan

Mercedes Unimog Germany

Bicycles

The first bicycle, called a hobbyhorse, was built about 150 years ago. It had a front wheel that could be turned but no pedals. Later, pedals were fixed to the front wheel to make the bicycle go faster.

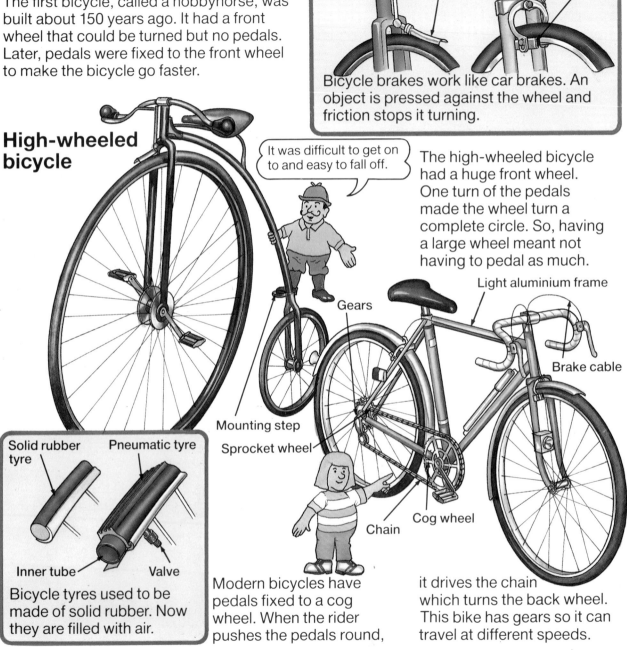

Spoon brake

Brake block

Bicycle brakes work like car brakes. An object is pressed against the wheel and friction stops it turning.

High-wheeled bicycle

It was difficult to get on to and easy to fall off.

The high-wheeled bicycle had a huge front wheel. One turn of the pedals made the wheel turn a complete circle. So, having a large wheel meant not having to pedal as much.

Light aluminium frame

Gears

Brake cable

Mounting step

Sprocket wheel

Solid rubber tyre

Pneumatic tyre

Inner tube

Valve

Bicycle tyres used to be made of solid rubber. Now they are filled with air.

Chain

Cog wheel

Modern bicycles have pedals fixed to a cog wheel. When the rider pushes the pedals round, it drives the chain which turns the back wheel. This bike has gears so it can travel at different speeds.

Motorbikes

The first motorbike was built about 120 years ago. It was a bicycle fitted with a steam engine. Now there are many different types of motorbike for different racing sports.

Road racing

A Grand Prix racing bike is the fastest bike built today. The engine is covered in so the bike can cut through the air.

Arrows show the movement of air over the bike.

The rider crouches forward so the wind rushes over him.

Sidecar racing

Low, streamlined shape

During a race, the passenger leans right out of the sidecar to balance it as it speeds round corners.

Trials bikes

Strong suspension

Trials riding is a cross-country competition which tests the skill of the rider. The bike has strong tyres to help it grip over rocks and through mud.

Dragbikes

Wide rear tyres (slicks).

Dragbikes have very powerful engines. The rider lies right across the bike so it travels faster through the wind.

Types of trains

The first railway tracks were built about 400 years ago, when animals were used to pull heavy loads along rails. At that time, the rails were made of wood.

The very first engines were driven by steam. Today trains are pulled by diesel engines and electric motors. On these pages you can see all three types.

Steam trains

American type 4-4-0

The American type 4-4-0 was one of the first steam trains to cross America.

The smokestack catches sparks from the fire.

Boiler

Bell

The tender carries wood for the fire.

60

How steam turns the wheels

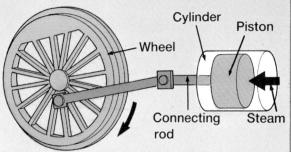

Cylinder

Piston

Wheel

Connecting rod

Steam

Burning coal or wood heats water in a large tank, called a boiler. Steam from the boiling water pushes pistons in a cylinder. The pistons are connected to the wheels.

Driving wheels power the train.

Leading wheels guide the train around bends.

Cowcatcher to push stray animals off the track.

Electric trains

Electric trains are the fastest in the world. They pick up electricity from overhead cables or from a third track on the ground.

Hikari express

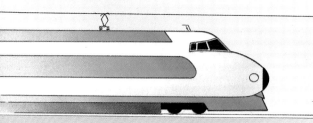

This Japanese train, nicknamed 'The Bullet' can travel at 209km/h (130mph).

Diesel trains

British Rail Inter-City 125

This train has a diesel engine. It is the same as a car engine but burns diesel oil instead of petrol. The diesel engine produces electricity in a generator. Electricity goes along cables to motors which turn the wheels and work the heaters and lights.

Underground railways

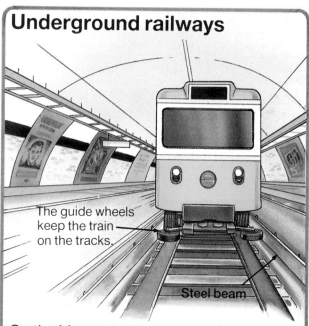

The guide wheels keep the train on the tracks.

Steel beam

On the Metro, the Paris underground, the trains run on pneumatic tyres. The trains are faster and quieter with rubber wheels.

The bogie

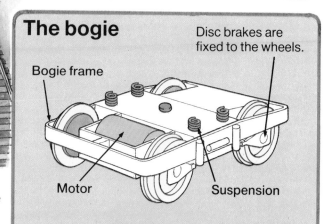

Disc brakes are fixed to the wheels.

Bogie frame

Motor

Suspension

The train carriages rest on top of bogies like this one. It lets the train bend as it goes around corners.

Trains today

Today's high speed trains are built for fast inter-city travel. This French TGV (Train à Grande Vitesse which means 'high speed train') has an average speed of 260km/h (161mph), which makes it the fastest passenger train in the world. A special track was built for it, without sharp bends and steep hills.

There are no signals on the TGV track for the driver to look for. Instead, electronic signals are sent to the driver's cab. They tell the driver what speed to travel.

The driver has a radio-telephone in the cab and there are emergency telephones beside the track every 1km (0.6 miles).

There is a locomotive carriage at each end of the train. This is what powers the train.

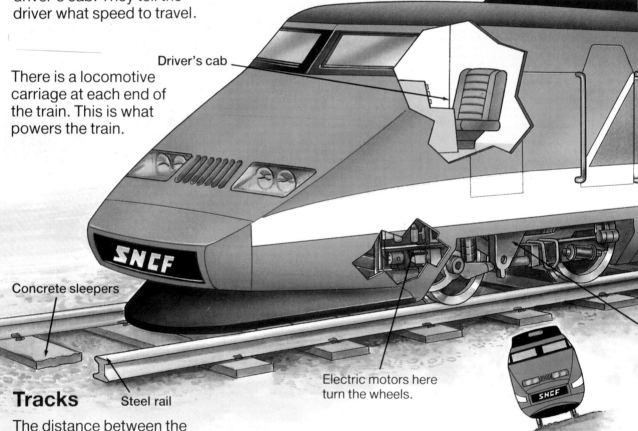

Driver's cab

Concrete sleepers

SNCF

Electric motors here turn the wheels.

Tracks

Steel rail

The distance between the two parallel tracks of a railway line is called the gauge. Throughout the world there is a standard gauge which is 1.43m (4ft 8½ inches).

The track is raised on one side so that the train can speed round corners.

44

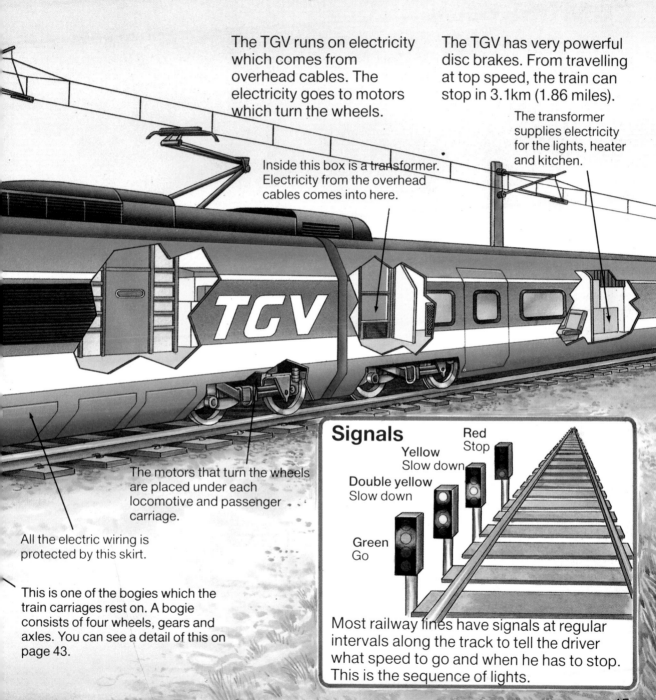

The TGV runs on electricity which comes from overhead cables. The electricity goes to motors which turn the wheels.

The TGV has very powerful disc brakes. From travelling at top speed, the train can stop in 3.1km (1.86 miles).

The transformer supplies electricity for the lights, heater and kitchen.

Inside this box is a transformer. Electricity from the overhead cables comes into here.

The motors that turn the wheels are placed under each locomotive and passenger carriage.

All the electric wiring is protected by this skirt.

This is one of the bogies which the train carriages rest on. A bogie consists of four wheels, gears and axles. You can see a detail of this on page 43.

Signals

Red
Stop

Yellow
Slow down

Double yellow
Slow down

Green
Go

Most railway lines have signals at regular intervals along the track to tell the driver what speed to go and when he has to stop. This is the sequence of lights.

45

Fastest on wheels

The first cars and motorbikes travelled very slowly. A hundred years ago, cars in Britain were only allowed to go at 6.4km/h (4mph). A man had to walk in front of the car to make sure the driver kept within the speed limit.

Fastest on the road

Aston Martin V8 Vantage

The Aston Martin V8 Vantage is one of the world's fastest and most powerful cars. It can accelerate from 0 to 161km/h (0 to 100mph) in just 11.9 seconds.

It has a top speed of 270km/h (168mph).

Car factories, like British Leyland, produce one car every six minutes. An Aston Martin takes 16 weeks to produce because each car is hand-built.

Fastest on rails

These trains are the fastest steam, diesel and electric trains in the world. They have all set speed records in the past and have been responsible for cutting down journey times between main cities. Here you can see how far each could travel in one hour.

Flying Scotsman (UK)   LNER Mallard (UK)

96km (60 miles)   161km (100 miles)

The Flying Scotsman was the first steam locomotive to provide a non-stop service from London to Edinburgh.

In 1938, Mallard set a new record for steam engines, travelling at 203km/h (126mph). No other steam train has travelled faster.

Kawasaki GPZ1000RX

The fastest motorbike on the road today is the Kawasaki GPZ1000. It can travel at over 260km/h (161mph).

The rider is protected from the wind by sleek panels. Holes in each side panel let cool air blow on to the engine to stop it from overheating.

World Land Speed Record

This is a test of speed run over a straight mile (1.6km). The vehicles competing must make one run in each direction within an hour.

Car class

Thrust 2, broke the speed record in 1983. The car travelled at an average speed of 1,019.4km/h (633.45mph).

Motorbike class

This very unusual motorbike, Lightning Bolt, broke the speed record in 1978, travelling at an average speed of 512.7km/h (318.59mph).

Inter-City 125 (UK)	Hikari express (Japan)	TGV (France)
200km (125miles)	210km (130miles)	260km (161 miles)

The Inter-City 125 is the fastest diesel train in the world. It can reach a top speed of 231km/h (143mph).

Japanese National Railways built a new track for this train which speeds along at over 210km/h (130mph).

This is the fastest train in the world. During tests it reached an amazing top speed of 390km/h (236mph).

Car words

Here are some special car words which have been used in this section of the book and others you will have heard of.

Petrol engine

Most cars burn petrol in their engines. A petrol engine has spark plugs which make an electric spark to ignite the petrol and run the engine.

Diesel engine

Most trucks and some cars have engines which burn diesel oil. This is a fuel like petrol. A diesel engine does not need spark plugs. Diesel vapour ignites by itself when it is squeezed into a very small space.

Turbo engine

A car with a turbo engine has extra power. It has a fan called a turbo fan. This blows more air and petrol vapour mix into the engine so more petrol is burned. This makes the car go faster.

Carburettor

The carburettor mixes petrol and air together to make petrol vapour. Petrol will not burn in the engine unless it is mixed with air.

Fuel injection

Many modern cars do not have a carburettor. Instead the petrol is sprayed into the cylinders in the engine, where it mixes with air. This is called fuel injection.

Chassis

The chassis is a steel frame which supports the car engine, gearbox and suspension. The car body is bolted on to the chassis.

Differential

The differential is a set of gears (cogged wheels) at the end of the driveshaft. These gears turn the rear axle and rear wheels, and they also let the wheels turn at different speeds when the car is travelling around corners. An ordinary car has one differential.

Four wheel drive (4WD)

Four wheel drive cars have two differentials. This means that the engine turns all four wheels.

THINGS THAT FLOAT

Annabel Thomas

Designed by Steve Page

Illustrated by Peter Bull

Contents

50	All about ships and boats		64	Things that skim
52	Steamboats		66	Submarines
54	Liners		68	Lifeboats
56	Boats and their engines		69	Fishing boats
58	Sailing boats		70	Biggest and fastest
60	Muscle power		71	Sea-way code
62	Cargo ships		72	Index

All about ships and boats

This section tells you all about ships and boats. You can find out how they float, what makes them go and what they do. It also tells you about some unusual ships and boats around the world, as well as those that have broken records for speed or size.

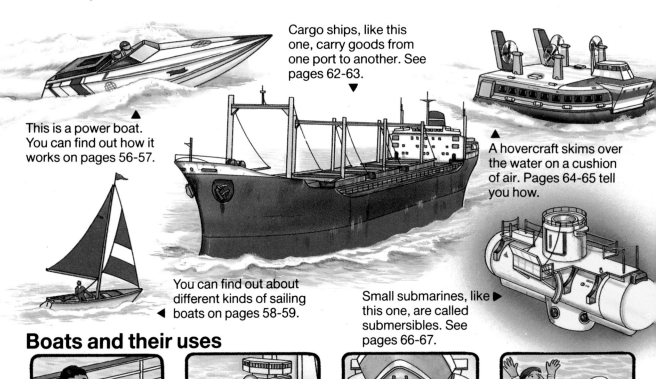

Cargo ships, like this one, carry goods from one port to another. See pages 62-63. ▼

This is a power boat. You can find out how it works on pages 56-57. ▲

A hovercraft skims over the water on a cushion of air. Pages 64-65 tell you how. ▲

You can find out about different kinds of sailing boats on pages 58-59. ◀

Small submarines, like ▶ this one, are called submersibles. See pages 66-67.

Boats and their uses

Some large ships, called liners, are built for holiday cruises. They are like floating hotels.

Huge naval ships have a runway on the deck where aircraft can take off and land.

Some ferries have ramps so cars, trucks and coaches can drive on and off them.

Lifeboats are specially built and equipped to save people from drowning at sea.

Floating and sinking

A big steel or wooden boat is very heavy. When it floats it pushes some of the water aside. The water round the boat pushes back. This push (force) of the water holds up the boat if the boat is not too heavy for its size.

A heavy boat needs to have high sides so lots of water can push against it.

Wood is light for its size and floats easily. ▼

Although metal is heavy, a steel ship can float. ▶

Hull

Because it is hollow, the metal shell or hull of a boat weighs less than a solid amount of metal of the same size. Both push aside the same amount of water, but the force of the water can support the weight of the hull because it is hollow.

Plasticine boat
Try this experiment.

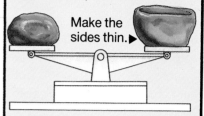

Make the sides thin. ▶

Take two pieces of plasticine of the same weight. Roll one into a ball and press out the other to make a cup-shaped boat.

Basin

Put them into some water. The ball sinks. Although both weigh the same, the "boat" floats as there is more water pushing it up.

Boat power

The earliest way of moving a boat along was by a person's muscles, using paddles or oars.

For thousands of years, sails were used to catch the wind and push the boat forward.

Now most large ships have diesel engines, but some use steam turbine engines.

Many modern submarines use nuclear power to turn steam turbines.

Steamboats

The first engines were invented at the end of the 18th century and were powered by steam. Here you can see an early steamboat engine. The steam is used to turn paddle-wheels either side of the boat. As they turn, they push against the water. This makes the boat move forward.

What is steam?

Steam is very hot and can burn you.

Steam is a gas which is made when water boils. You can see the powerful way it spouts from a boiling kettle. It is this power which works a steam-engine.

Steamships

Savannah

In 1819, the first sailing ship with an engine crossed the Atlantic. An American ship, *Savannah*, only used its engines for 8 hours of the 21 day journey.

Sirius

The first steamship to make a crossing without using its sails was the British ship, *Sirius*, built in 1837. It took 18 days.

1. Coal is burnt to heat water in the boiler.

2. The steam is piped from the boiler into a cylinder.

3. As steam enters the first cylinder, the piston is pushed up, turning the crankshaft.

The turning paddles dip into the water, moving the boat along.

Paddle-wheel

Steam

Boiler

Cylinder

Piston

Escaping steam

Crankshaft

4. A small hole lets the steam escape so the piston can fall back down again.

5. The first piston goes down while steam enters the second cylinder, pushing its piston up.

6. The up and down movement of the pistons turns the crankshaft which turns the paddle-wheels.

Screw propulsion

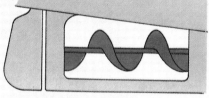

Early type of screw propeller.

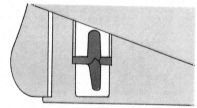

Later type of screw propeller.

In the 1840s screw propellers were invented and fitted to the back of boats. Although they were smaller than paddle-wheels they made the boat go faster. Like paddle-wheels, they were powered by steam engines and were turned by the spinning motion of the crankshaft.

During the trial run of a boat, the end of a long screw propeller broke off. It worked better so propellers were made shorter.

How propellers work

The *Great Britain* was the first iron ship to use a screw propeller rather than paddle-wheels.

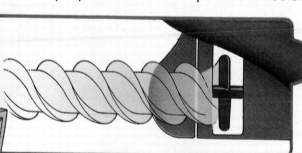

Propellers work by going through the water like a corkscrew goes through a cork. As the blades of the propeller turn, the water is forced backwards. This thrusts the boat forwards.

Steam turbines

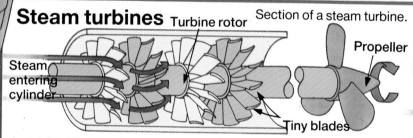

Turbine rotor

Section of a steam turbine.

Steam entering cylinder

Propeller

Tiny blades

Turbinia

Some liners are still powered by huge steam turbines.

In 1894 Sir Charles Parsons invented the steam turbine. It turned faster and so produced greater speeds.

The hundreds of tiny blades turn with the turbine rotor as steam rushes past. This turns the propeller.

Turbinia was the first turbine powered boat. It was launched in 1897 and had three turbines and three propellers.

Liners

Liners are very big ships. In the past people had to travel by ship if they wanted to go to another country. Nowadays aeroplanes take much of the passenger traffic and liners are used mostly for holiday cruises.

The biggest passenger liner in use is the *Queen Elizabeth II*, or *QE2*. It is like a small city, with shops, restaurants, cinema and even a hospital.

These are kennels where passengers can keep their pets.

This is the ship's theatre.

In the ship's shopping centre, passengers can buy things, such as clothes, food and flowers.

The *QE2*

There are four swimming pools.

Tennis court

The *QE2* has two propellers, each with six blades.

The ship's health club is here.

This is the ship's launderette.

Measuring speed

At sea, speed is measured in knots. The name comes from the time when a sailor would throw the end of a knotted line into sea. As the ship moved forward, the line unravelled and the knots, which were equally spaced, were counted over a period of time.

This is the ship's control room – a huge computer works out its speed and direction.

This is the turbine room, where all the ship's diesel powered turbine engines are.

The average travelling speed of the *QE2* is 28½ knots.

Nowadays a knot is a speed of one nautical mile per hour. A nautical (sea) mile is different from a land mile. It is 1852 metres, so a knot is 1.85 kilometres an hour (1.15 miles an hour).

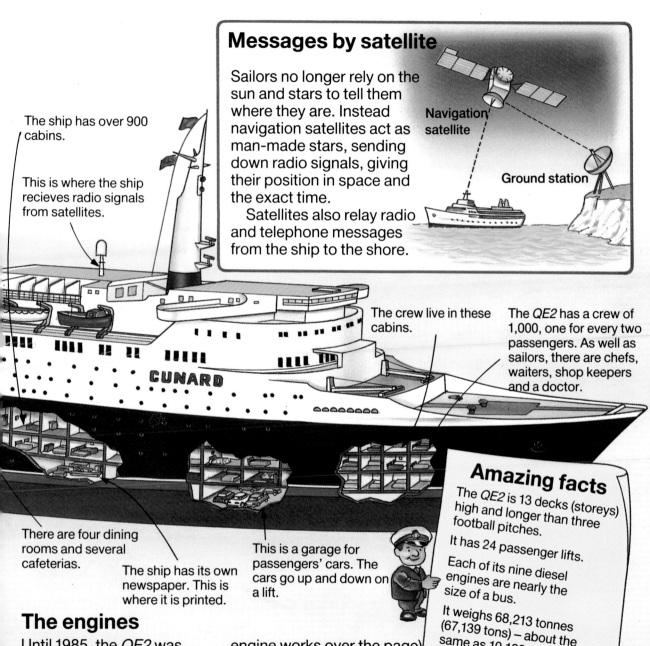

Messages by satellite

Sailors no longer rely on the sun and stars to tell them where they are. Instead navigation satellites act as man-made stars, sending down radio signals, giving their position in space and the exact time.

Satellites also relay radio and telephone messages from the ship to the shore.

Navigation satellite

Ground station

The ship has over 900 cabins.

This is where the ship recieves radio signals from satellites.

The crew live in these cabins.

The QE2 has a crew of 1,000, one for every two passengers. As well as sailors, there are chefs, waiters, shop keepers and a doctor.

CUNARD

There are four dining rooms and several cafeterias.

The ship has its own newspaper. This is where it is printed.

This is a garage for passengers' cars. The cars go up and down on a lift.

Amazing facts

The QE2 is 13 decks (storeys) high and longer than three football pitches.

It has 24 passenger lifts.

Each of its nine diesel engines are nearly the size of a bus.

It weighs 68,213 tonnes (67,139 tons) – about the same as 10,100 elephants.

Each cabin has a direct satellite telephone link to anywhere in the world.

The engines

Until 1985, the QE2 was powered by steam turbine engines. In 1986 nine diesel powered engines were fitted (you can find out how a diesel engine works over the page). Its new engines are much cleaner than the old ones and enable the ship to move faster than before.

Boats and their engines

Most small boats have a petrol engine fixed at the back. They are called outboard motors because the engine can be lifted off the boat. Larger boats have powerful diesel engines, housed inside the hull. They are called inboard motors.

This boat is called a power boat. It has two diesel engines and two propellers.

Panel showing boat's speed and how much fuel there is.

Steering wheel

Deck

Each engine is protected by a case.

Long, narrow hull for racing.

The engine
A diesel engine, like a petrol engine, is called an internal combustion engine. This means the fuel is burnt inside the engine. You can see how on the next page.

Pilot boats
Pilot boats take sea pilots to large ships. The pilot then guides the ship through dangerous and unfamiliar water.

Motor cruisers
Motor cruisers are often big boats, with living quarters on board. They are used for cruising holidays.

Tenders
A tender, such as this one, is kept aboard large ocean liners for carrying passengers from the ship to the shore.

The diesel engine

The diesel engine was invented by a German, Dr Rudolph Diesel, in 1897. It uses a special type of fuel called diesel oil.

A boat engine can have between two and twelve cylinders. The more cylinders an engine has, the greater its power.

This engine has four cylinders. Each cylinder shows one of four things that happen to turn the propeller.

2. The valve closes and the piston moves up, squashing the air. This makes the air very hot.

3. The injector squirts fuel into the hot air. The mixture explodes, pushing the piston down.

1. Air enters the cylinder through the inlet valve and the piston moves down.

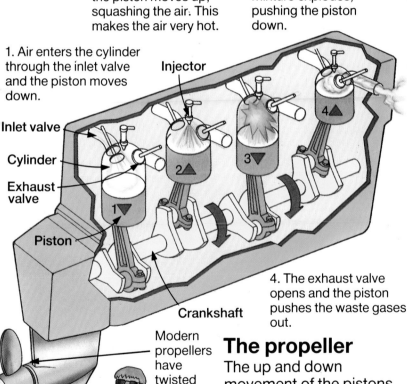

Injector

Inlet valve

Cylinder

Exhaust valve

Piston

Crankshaft

Modern propellers have twisted blades.

4. The exhaust valve opens and the piston pushes the waste gases out.

The propeller

The up and down movement of the pistons turns the crankshaft which turns the propeller. Its blades push the water backwards and the boat is driven forwards.

Power boat racing

Power boats are designed specially for racing. The fastest have jet engines, the kind of engine an aeroplane uses.

A famous racing event is the Bahamas Powerboat Grand-Prix.

Record breaker

It took 3 days, 8 hours and 31 minutes to cross a distance of over 5,000 km (3,000 miles).

In 1986, a British power boat, *Virgin Atlantic Challenger*, crossed the Atlantic in record time. It won the Blue Riband, previously awarded to liners for the fastest Atlantic crossing.

Sailing boats

For thousands of years boats with sails have relied on the power of the wind to push them along. The sails "catch" the wind and the force of the wind pushing against the sails moves the boat forward.

An arrangement of sails is called a rig. You can find out about the development of rigs on the opposite page.

The first sails

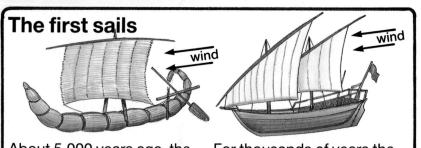

About 5,000 years ago, the Egyptians used square sails. When the wind blew from behind the boat was pushed forward.

For thousands of years the Arabs used triangular (lateen) sails. They used ropes to curve the sails round to catch the wind.

The mainsail is joined to the boom and mast.

The jib is an extra sail which catches the wind. It helps to steer the boat and turn it round.

Nowadays most sails are made of a light, waterproof material.

Modern sails are triangular with a curved outside edge. This style is called Bermudan.

Small yachts like this sailing dinghy only use a mainsail and a smaller sail, called the jib.

Steering the boat

The boat is steered by the tiller, which acts like a steering wheel. The tiller is joined to the rudder which changes the direction of the boat.

When the tiller is moved to the right, it moves the rudder and the boat turns left. When it is moved to the left, the boat goes right.

The centreboard keeps the boat going straight. It helps to stop the boat drifting sideways, when the wind pushes on the sails.

Mainsail

Jib

Mast

Boom

Tiller

Rudder

Centreboard

Hull

The catamaran

The trimaran

A catamaran has two hulls and a trimaran has a central hull with two smaller hulls either side. Both have less boat in the water than an ordinary boat and so they float high in the water. They skim over the water and can go very fast.

Tacking

Sail

Direction of wind

If a sailor wants to go in the direction the wind is blowing from, he steers in a zig-zag. This is called tacking. On each part of the zig-zag the wind is blowing on the side of the sails and pushes the boat forwards.

The America's Cup

The America's Cup is a yachting event which takes place every four years in the country of the last winner. In 1986-87 the races were held in Australia and were won by the American yacht *Stars and Stripes*.

America's Cup trophy

Story of rigs

Chinese ship

In the 9th century, Chinese ships were built with several masts and sails made of bamboo matting. This design lasted for hundreds of years.

Three-masted ship

In the 15th century, three-masted ships were built in Europe. These ships were used for sea battles, exploring and trade.

Clipper

In the 1820s cargo ships called Clippers were made. They had many large sails, a long slim hull and could go very fast.

Muscle power

Long ago people used their hands like paddles to propel their boats along. Then they made wooden paddles which were bigger than their hands and worked better.

Later long oars were used, like the ones in the picture. These worked even more efficiently.

Rowing boats like this one are made from very light but strong material, such as fibreglass.

The cox shouts instructions to the crew and steers the boat.

Racing crews often practise several hours a day to make sure they work well together to make the boat go faster.

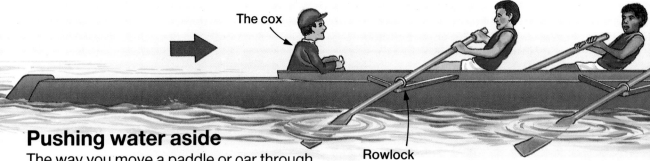

The cox

Rowlock

Pushing water aside

The way you move a paddle or oar through water is similar to the way you move your arms when you swim. As the paddle or oar pushes the water backwards, the boat moves forwards.

Each oar rests on a rowlock, so the oar works like a lever.

Ships with oars

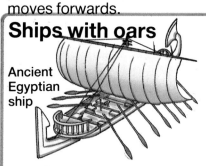

Ancient Egyptian ship

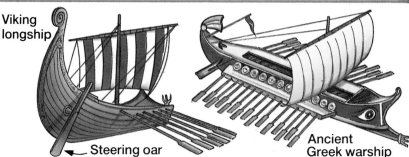

Viking longship

Steering oar

Ancient Greek warship

As long as 5,000 years ago, the Egyptians rowed their ships along with oars when there was no wind or it was blowing the wrong way.

About 800 years ago, the people of Scandinavia, called Vikings, built long, narrow ships, called longships. They had up to 25 oars on each side.

The oars of an Ancient Greek warship were usually arranged on different levels so that the oarsmen did not get in each other's way.

Going faster

People soon discovered that the length of the oars was important. A single pull on a long oar pushes the boat further forward than a single pull on a short oar.

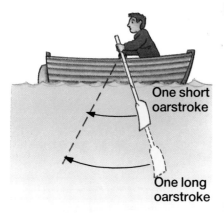

One short oarstroke

One long oarstroke

The boat's streamlined shape enables it to travel through the water at great speed.

Canoeing

Protective helmet

Double ended paddle

A type of canoe is still used in some countries, such as Alaska, for fishing and transport. Mostly, canoes are used for sporting events, such as the slalom. Competitors have to weave their canoe in and out of a row of poles in fast flowing water, without hitting them.

Unusual boats

Gondola

Gondolas are boats used on the canals of Venice in Italy. A gondolier stands at the back of the boat, propelling it along with one long oar.

Punt

Flat bottomed boats called punts are used for pleasure. A long pole is pushed against the river bed to propel the punt along.

Reed boat

Boats made of reeds are still used in some countries round the world, such as Peru in South America. People use long poles to push the boat along.

Cargo ships

Cargo ships carry goods, or cargo, from one port to another. The cargo can be anything from oranges to steel rods or coal to wheat.

A port has roads and railways to bring cargo to the ship. It also has huge warehouses where cargo can be stored before being loaded or unloaded on to or off a ship.

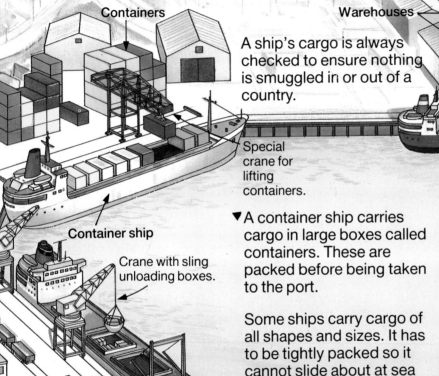

Containers

Warehouses

A ship's cargo is always checked to ensure nothing is smuggled in or out of a country.

Special crane for lifting containers.

Container ship

Crane with sling unloading boxes.

Grain being piped down a chute.

▼ A container ship carries cargo in large boxes called containers. These are packed before being taken to the port.

Some ships carry cargo of all shapes and sizes. It has to be tightly packed so it cannot slide about at sea ◀ and be damaged.

▲ Some ships carry bulk food, such as sugar or wheat. It is poured down chutes into the ship and sucked out again by pipes.

Roll on/roll off ships are built so loaded lorries and trains can drive straight on and off the ship, without delay.
▼

Roll on/roll off ship

Railway

Road

62

Oil tankers

Very big ships that carry oil are called supertankers. They are too large for most docks so the oil is piped to storage tanks from special terminals outside the port.

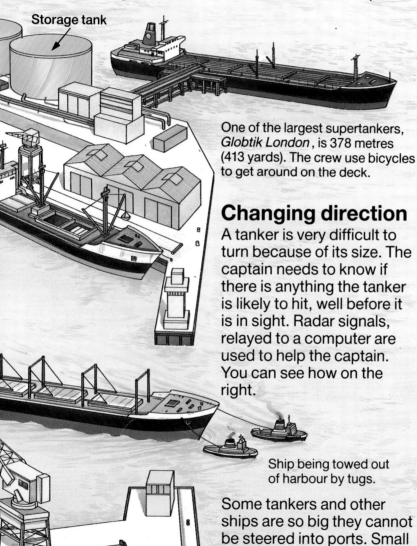

Storage tank

One of the largest supertankers, *Globtik London*, is 378 metres (413 yards). The crew use bicycles to get around on the deck.

Changing direction

A tanker is very difficult to turn because of its size. The captain needs to know if there is anything the tanker is likely to hit, well before it is in sight. Radar signals, relayed to a computer are used to help the captain. You can see how on the right.

Ship being towed out of harbour by tugs.

Some tankers and other ships are so big they cannot be steered into ports. Small boats, called tugs, tow them in and out of the docks, and put them into position.

Using computers

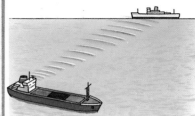

Tankers send out signals, called radar, to look for ships and rocks. Radar travels through the air until it "hits" something.

The signals bounce back to a radar screen. The tanker's computer works out how fast and in which direction the ship must go to avoid a collision.

Computer sails

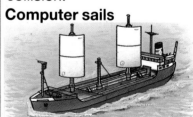

Shin Aitoku Maru

The Japanese tanker, *Shin Aitoku Maru,* has special metal sails to push it along. A computer works out when the sails should be turned to catch the wind.

Things that skim

A hovercraft is a type of boat that skims over water or land supported by a cushion of air. It is sometimes called an air-cushion vehicle or ACV.

There are two other types of boats that skim over the water. They are the hydrofoil and the jetfoil. You can find out about them on the opposite page.

The hovercraft

The propellers spin pushing the hovercraft forwards.

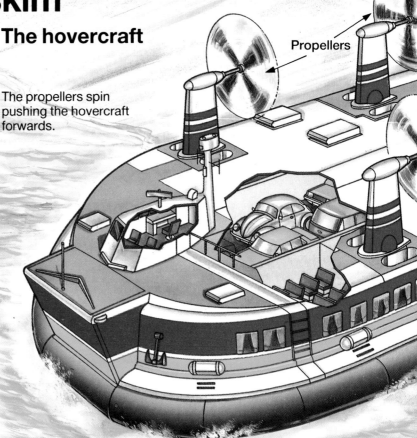

Propellers

Floating on air

Yoghurt pot

Air

Polystyrene tray

To test how a hovercraft works, cut the bottom out of a yoghurt pot. Then cut a hole in the middle of a polystyrene tray big enough to put the yoghurt pot in. If you blow into the pot, the tray will move easily on a cushion of air.

Steering the hovercraft

The propellers move round to steer the hovercraft and the rudders move to one side or the other when it changes direction.

A hovercraft keeps steady in rough water as the skirt can move up and down or bulge out when the waves push the cushion about.

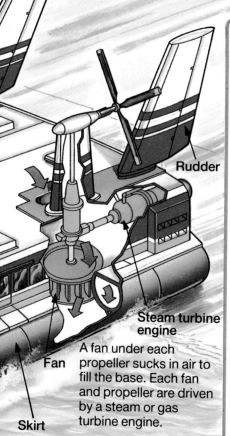

Rudder

Steam turbine engine

Fan A fan under each propeller sucks in air to fill the base. Each fan and propeller are driven by a steam or gas turbine engine.

Skirt A rubber skirt fitted round the base stops the cushion of air escaping.

Stopping at the port

A hovercraft comes out of the water. The engines are turned off and as no air goes into the skirt it sinks to rest on its base.

The hydrofoil

A hydrofoil is a boat that has underwater wings (called hydrofoils). The whole boat lifts out of the water as it gathers speed.

How a hydrofoil works

The top surface of the wings of a hydrofoil are smooth, so water quickly runs off them. The wings rise up, lifting the whole boat out of the water. There is then no water to push against the boat so it can go very fast.

V-foils

Some hydrofoils have V shaped wings, called V-foils. They stick out of the water on both sides of the boat as it goes faster.

Submerged foils

Submerged foils stay under the water so the hydrofoil looks as if it has legs. They can change direction to suit different weather conditions.

The Jetfoil

A jetfoil is a type of hydrofoil. It is propelled forwards by two water jets. Gas turbines work the pumps which force the water through holes under great pressure to make the jets.

Direction of water

Submarines

Submarines travel under the sea. They are powered by diesel engines or nuclear powered turbines. A nuclear submarine, like the one in this picture, has a rounder hull than a submarine with a diesel engine. Nuclear submarines can work for years without needing to be refuelled and can stay under water for as long as two years without coming to the surface.

Radio antennae
The radio antennae pick up satellite messages.

The periscope
A periscope is a tube with a mirror at both ends. When it is raised a sailor in the submarine can see what is happening above the water while the rest of the submarine is below the water.

Hydroplanes

Conning tower
The submarine is steered from the conning tower.

Sonar detector
The sonar detector picks up sound waves (see opposite page).

Double hull

Ballast tanks

Control room

Sleeping quarters

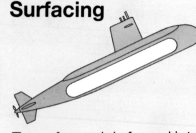

Diving

Ballast tank

Before the submarine dives, shutters are opened so the sea floods into the ballast tanks and the submarine sinks.

Underwater

Once under the water, the level of water in the ballast tanks is adjusted so the submarine stays at a chosen depth.

Surfacing

To surface, air is forced into the ballast tanks under great pressure. This forces out the water and the submarine rises.

Propeller

The propeller make the submarine go forwards.

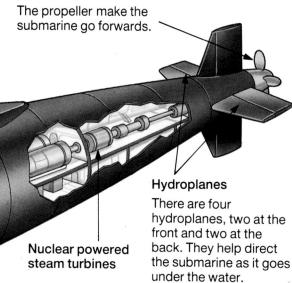

Hydroplanes

There are four hydroplanes, two at the front and two at the back. They help direct the submarine as it goes under the water.

Nuclear powered steam turbines

Submarines have a double hull. Between its two walls are ballast tanks – tanks that are filled with water to make the submarine sink.

Sonar

Sonar is a way of finding out where other ships and submarines are from the sounds they make. There are two kinds of sonar, Active and Passive.

Active sonar

The submarine sends out sound waves. When they hit something they "ping" and an echo bounces back to the submarine.

Passive sonar

Passive sonar picks up the smallest sound using electronic equipment. It makes no sound so the submarine's presence is secret.

The *Turtle*

The first submarine was built by an American in the late 18th century. It was shaped like an egg and had no engines.

Nautilus

In 1958, an American submarine, *Nautilus,* was the first vessel to reach the North Pole. It travelled there under the ice.

The Bathyscaphe

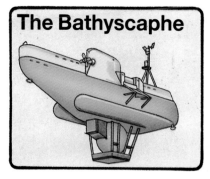

The Bathyscaphe is a submersible (small submarine) designed specially for very deep underwater research.

Lifeboats

Bad weather at sea often causes accidents and shipwrecks. Lifeboats are designed to go out in strong winds and rough seas, and their crews are trained to rescue people in danger of drowning.

Padded jacket
Waterproof padded jacket is worn for warmth. It is brightly coloured to show up against the sea.

Waterproof trousers

Lifejacket
Lifejacket, filled with air, keeps a person afloat in the sea.

Bump cap
The bump cap and hood protects the head.

Inflatables

Inflatable lifeboats rescue people close to the shore.

Getting the right way up

1

2 Superstructure

The superstructure has watertight doors.

3

If a lifeboat capsizes, it can come back up again within a few seconds. This is called self-righting. A lifeboat does not sink because air is trapped inside the superstructure (the top of the boat). The weight of the heavy engines in the bottom of the boat then pulls the hull back into the water, so the boat is the right way up again.

Fishing boats

Fishing boats, called trawlers, have enormous nets, called trawls. This trawler is called a purse seiner. Its net circles the fish and is drawn in by a rope before being winched aboard.

Purse seiner

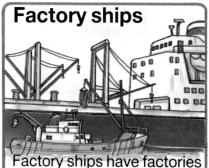

Factory ships have factories on board where the fish are cleaned and prepared for sale. Often smaller fishing boats off-load their haul onto factory ships at sea.

The fish are sent along big square pipes to huge, square trays. Here, a factory worker cleans and prepares the fish.

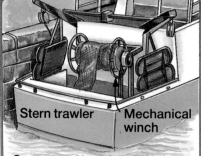

Stern trawler   Mechanical winch

Stern trawlers haul their nets in from the stern (back of the boat). They are hauled in by mechanical winch.

On board

Once on board, the fish is either packed with ice in boxes or put in huge freezers. Ships with freezers can stay at sea for a long time, without the fish going bad.

Some ships even have fish factories on board. You can find out about them on the right.

Some prepared fish are stored in barrels and then stacked on the ship's deck. Others are packed in trays and frozen.

Biggest and fastest

On this page you can find out about some of the world's biggest and fastest ships. Many of them are naval ships. Some are so big that they have runways on deck where aeroplanes can land and take off.

The biggest

Apart from some tankers, the biggest ships to have been built are three United States' Navy aircraft carriers called *Nimitz*, *Dwight D. Eisenhower* and *Carl Vinson*. Each weighs 92,869 tonnes (91,374 tons).

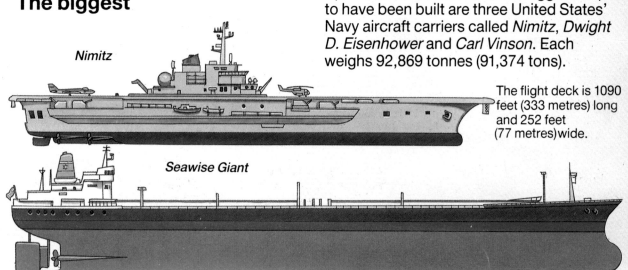

Nimitz

The flight deck is 1090 feet (333 metres) long and 252 feet (77 metres) wide.

Seawise Giant

The biggest oil tanker is called *Seawise Giant*. It is owned by Liberia, though it was built in Japan. It weighs 564,733 tonnes (555,697 tons) and is 1,504 feet (458 metres) long. It is so long that *Nimitz* is only two thirds its length.

The fastest

SS United States

The fastest passenger liner was the *SS United States*. On its first voyage in 1952, it crossed the Atlantic at a speed of 35.59 knots (66 km/h, 41 mph).

Le Terrible

A French destroyer (a light, fast warship), called *Le Terrible*, built in 1935 could travel as fast as 45.25 knots (83.9 km/h, 52.1 mph).

In 1967 an updated *Bluebird* overturned having reached a speed of 527 km/h (327 mph).

Bluebird

In 1956, *Bluebird*, a jet-propelled speedboat, got up a speed of more than 360 km/h (223 mph), on an English lake. This is the world water speed record.

Sea-way code

At sea, there are rules that ships and boats have to obey, just as cars have to obey rules when on the road. Sailors learn to read signs and signals from other ships, lighthouses and buoys. Even though nowadays ships send messages by radio, sailors still learn all the old rules of the sea.

Lighthouse

Lighthouses

Lighthouses are built on rocky headlands. Their lights warn ships and boats to keep clear. They are also built at sea, to mark rocks and reefs.

Lightships

A lightship is used in an area where it is impossible to build a lighthouse, for instance on a sandbank.

Lightship

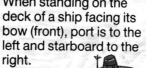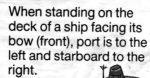

When standing on the deck of a ship facing its bow (front), port is to the left and starboard to the right.

Starboard

Port

Port

Starboard

Buoys

Buoys mark areas that might be dangerous for boats, such as hidden rocks, channels or even wrecks of ships. Their positions are also marked on charts of the sea.

Buoy

Keep to the right

One of the international rules of the sea is to keep to the right. This rule stops ships and boats crashing into each other. These two ships are both going to the right, otherwise they would collide.

Both ships must also give one short blast on a siren.

Sea signals

Nowadays most ships send out radio signals to tell other ships of their whereabouts. They can also make strong blasts on a siren when it is foggy.

71

Boat words

Below are some special words describing parts of a ship or boat. You will have come across most of them in this section of the book.

Bow

The bow is the front end of a ship or boat.

Centreboard

The centreboard is a flat, dagger-shaped board which projects through the bottom of a boat. It can be raised or lowered. A fixed board on the bottom of a boat is called a keel.

Chart

A chart is a map of a sea area. It shows such things as coastlines, rocks and the position of buoys and lighthouses. It also tells you how deep the sea is in different places.

Foil

A foil is the name of the underwater wing of a hydrofoil. This is a type of boat which lifts out of the water on its wings.

Hull

The hull is the body or shell of a boat or ship, consisting of its upper deck, sides and bottom.

Knot

A knot is the speed of one nautical (sea) mile per hour. One nautical mile is equal to 1,853 metres (6,080 feet).

Mast

The mast is a tall upright pole to which a boat's sails are attached.

Port

Port is the left hand side of a boat, when you are facing towards the front or bow of the boat.

Propeller

A propeller looks like a fan attached to the back of a boat. When the propeller turns, its blades push the water backwards which thrusts the boat forwards.

Rig

A rig is the arrangement of masts, sails and ropes on a boat or ship.

Rudder

A rudder is a paddle-shaped steering board at the back of a boat or ship. When moved to the right, the boat goes to the left. When moved to the left, the boat goes to the right.

Starboard

Starboard is the right hand side of the boat when you are facing towards the front, or bow of the boat.

Stern

The stern is the back end of a ship or boat.

Tiller

The tiller is a handle joined to the rudder of a small sailing boat. It acts like a steering wheel. When turned to the left, it moves the rudder and the boat goes right. When turned to the right, the boat goes left.

First published in 1987 by Usborne Publishing Ltd, 20 Garrick Street, London WC2E 9BJ, England.   Printed in Belgium.   © 1987 Usborne Publishing Ltd.

Index

aerofoil, 4, 12, 35
aileron, 3
airship,
    blimp, 3, 15
    Zeppelin, 15, 22
airport, 10-11
axle,
    front, 39
    rear, 20, 29, 31

ballast tanks, 66, 57
bathyscaphe, 67
bicycle,
    high-wheeled, 26, 40
    hobbyhorse, 39
    modern, 39
bi-plane, 2, 18
boom, 58
brakes,
    block, 40
    cable, 40
    disc, 33
    drum, 33
    duct, 35
    shoe, 30
    spoon, 40
    pad, 33
buoy, 71

canoe, 61
carburettor, 30
cars,
    Ford Anglia, 37
    Formula 1, 27, 35
    Land Rover, 38
    Mercedes Unimog, 39
    Peugeot, 205, 37
    Subaru, 29

catamaran, 59
centreboard, 58
chassis, 28
clipper, 59
connecting rod, 30
container ship, 59
control tower, 10
cox, 60
crankshaft, 30
cylinder, 30, 42

differential,
    front, 39
    rear, 28, 29, 31
driveshaft, 28, 29, 30

elevator, 3
engine,
    diesel, 43, 51, 54, 55, 56, 57, 66
    internal combustion (petrol) 27, 30-31
    jet, 2, 6, 8-9
    rocket, 2, 20
    steam, 27, 42, 51, 52, 53, 55, 67
    turbofan, 6, 9
    turbojet, 9
    turboprop, 9
    turboshaft, 9

factory ship, 69
ferry, 51
fishing boat, 69
flight deck, 7
flight plan, 11
float-sea plane, 18
four wheel drive, 38-39

gears,
    car, 31, 32, 33
    bicycle, 40
glider, 2, 15
gondola, 61
gravity, 21

hang gliding, 3, 17
helicopter, 2, 13, 22
    air-sea rescue, 13
    crane, 13
    crop spraying, 13
hot-air balloon, 2, 14
hovercraft, 50, 64-65
hydroplane, 66, 67

jet,
    Boeing 747, 6-7, 9, 22
    Concorde, 7, 9, 22
    Harrier jump jet, 13
    Heinkel He 178, 8
jetfoil, 64, 65

knot, 54, 70

lifeboat, 50, 68
lighter-than-air craft, 2, 14-15
lightship, 71
liner, 50, 52
longboat, Viking, 60

mast, 58, 59
motorbike, 47
motor cruiser, 56

nautical mile, 54

oar, 60, 61
orbit, 21

paddle-wheel, 52, 53
parachuting, 17
pilot boat, 56
piston, 30, 42
pit stop, 34
port, 62, 70
power boat, 50, 57
propeller, 4, 8, 18, 53, 54,
    56, 57, 64, 65, 67

radar, 24, 63
radiator (car), 28, 30, 31
railway,
    gauge, 44
    tracks, 42
reed boat, 61
rocket, 2, 20
rotor blade, 12
rowing, 58-59
rudder, 3, 13, 18, 58, 64, 65

sail, 58, 63
    Bermudan, 58
    computer, 63
    jib, 58
    lanteen, 58
    mainsail, 58
    square, 58
satellite, 3, 21, 54, 55
seaplane, 18
sonar, 66, 67
space flight, 19, 20-21
Space Shuttle, 21
spark plug, 30
spoiler, 3, 5
starboard, 71
steamboat, 52-53
submarine, 50-51, 66, 67

tanker, oil, 63, 70
tender, 56
thermal, 2, 17
tiller, 58
train,
    diesel, 43, 46
    electric, 43, 45, 46
    signals, 44, 45
    steam, 27, 42, 46

trawler, 69
trials bike, 41
trimaran, 59
tug, 63
turbine, 51, 53, 55, 65, 67
tyres,
    slicks, 36
    pneumatic, 27, 40

VTOL (Vertical take-off and
    landing), 12

wheels,
    cogged, 32, 33, 40
    driving, 42
    leading, 42
    steering, 29
wings,
    delta, 7
    straight, 7
    swept, 7
World Land Speed Record, 47

First published in 1987 by
Usborne Publishing Ltd,
20 Garrick Street,
London WC2E 9BJ,
England.

© 1987 Usborne Publishing Ltd.